Make Something of It

THE **SHARP** SISTERS

#1
Make Something of It

STEPHANIE PERRY MOORE

darbycreek
MINNEAPOLIS

Darby Creek
A division of Lerner Publishing Group, Inc.
241 First Avenue North
Minneapolis, MN 55401 USA

For reading levels and more information, look up this title at www.lernerbooks.com.

The images in this book are used with the permission of:
Front Cover: © Andreas Kuehn/Iconica/Getty Images;
© SeanPavonePhoto/Shutterstock.com (background).

Main body text set in Janson Text LT Std 12/17.
Typeface provided by Linotype AG.

Library of Congress Cataloging-in-Publication Data

Moore, Stephanie Perry.
    #1 Make something of it / by Stephanie Perry Moore.
      pages   cm. — (The Sharp sisters)
      Summary: After witnessing abusive high school and adult relationships, seventeen-year-old Shelby must decide how to respond, especially considering that one of the abuse women is the wife of the man opposing Shelby's father in the mayoral race.
      ISBN 978-1-4677-3722-7 (lib. bdg. : alk. paper)
      ISBN 978-1-4677-4657-1 (eBook)
      [1. Abused women—Fiction. 2. Dating violence—Fiction. 3. High schools—Fiction. 4. Schools—Fiction. 5. Family life—Fiction] I. Title.
PZ7.M788125Mai 2014
[Fic]—dc23   2013040856

Manufactured in the United States of America
1 – SB – 7/15/14

For
Jackie Dixon

If I had sisters, you'd be one I'd choose.
Even as my college roommate,
you have always taught me to push to
be great.
I love your strength and your heart.
May every reader be a go-getter and
care as deeply as you do.

You're at a new chapter. I know you'll
make it great ... I love you!

CHAPTER ONE
STRANGER

"Shelby Grace Sharp, you keep looking at yourself in this mirror like what you see is going to miraculously change," I said to myself with attitude, wishing and hoping for a different outcome.

It wasn't that I thought I was ugly or anything. I just wasn't quite happy with my life. It feels like the weight of the world is always on my shoulders. I'm the oldest of five girls, and I guess you can say we're spoiled. None of us have to share a room. We live in a freakin' mansion, and we have a maid and a cook. Honestly, we want for nothing.

Our parents are still together and have been married for twenty years. My dad is a former NFL player, who now is an attorney in a thriving private practice, and my mom is no slouch. She's an attorney too who works for the State of North Carolina. All the legislators go through her to get their policies tight. Life was good flying under the radar, but now my dad is changing the game. He's running for mayor, and everything we do, everywhere we go, every word we say is scrutinized.

I'm not a star, but I'm sick and tired of the paparazzi. I'm not trying to kill myself or anything, so why do the tabloids seem to only print bad stuff? My life's not that bad, yet I'm not a happy girl with all this pressure to be perfect. And I'll be daggonit, I'm going to snap on the next person who says something to me.

"You tied that scarf around your neck five different ways," a dude said from out of nowhere, but I didn't have to turn around to see him.

I looked over my shoulder in the mirror, and the sight I saw stunned me. I was five six and 125 pounds. This guy had to be six feet with muscles I could see bulging from his white shirt. But why was he all in my business? And why was he walking closer? I turned around and put my hand on his chest, and it felt like a brick, but I didn't let him know I liked the touch.

"You're just like my mom. Thinking what you see is going to change if you stare in the mirror long enough. It is what it is, girl. You better make something of it."

"You act like I asked your opinion."

He bowed like a waiter, "Pardon me. I was simply saying you've got gorgeous, caramel-brown skin that glows. Your sassy, sharp, short hairdo says, 'You better watch me.' Your bold, light mocha eyes command attention, and your smile is perfectly alluring. Do you not see all that in the mirror? 'Cause if you don't see that, you're blind."

Was he serious? I was caught off guard with his strong description. Was he coming on to me, or was he playing me? Either way he was too close, and I had to back up.

We were backstage at the largest theater in Charlotte, in a greenroom. I knew he was full of it when he started giving a sly grin. The smart aleck who was waving a white cloth napkin in his hands needed to get back to work and leave me alone. Yeah, he was cute but certainly not my type. I didn't need a boyfriend anyway. I had one more year in high school, and I'd be out of here. I needed to stay focused on me and clearly figure out what I want. The scarf he was talking about me tying five different ways was my new creation. It was a scart—a scarf and belt in one.

I know my dad said he wanted to change the city of Charlotte and make this world a better place and all, but I hated that he needed us to play a precious sweet family to help him win. I mean, we didn't have a bunch of issues. Even with a bunch of women under one roof, we pretty much got along. But who wanted to be heading into her senior year with life upside down?

It was bad enough that I was going to have to change high schools. Yup, there was a big scandal at my school last year. It was a private, Christian school, and the pastor was under scrutiny and charged with having sex with minors. As a result, everybody started taking their kids out of there. A teacher started telling the wrong people how the school was taking shortcuts, and the next thing you know, we lost our accreditation. There are two other private schools I'd had my eye on for a long time, so I should be okay with completing my senior year somewhere new. I just wish I knew the outcome of this mayoral race. I liked things to be in order, and right now with this campaign, things were anything but in order.

"Shelby, there you are," my mom said, as if they'd been looking all over the world for me.

"I haven't moved since y'all left, Mom."

"I know, but I thought you were following us. Help your sisters tie those scarves. Everybody's got them going different ways."

"It's not a scarf, Mom. It's a scart—a scarf-belt," I said brazenly, wanting her to use the right name for my design.

My dad's colors were royal blue and black. He was a Democrat. The scarts shamelessly displayed those colors.

"Daddy's opponents are chumps," my outspoken, younger sister Sloan said.

Slade, Sloan, and I looked like sisters. We looked like my mom. Brown skin, mocha eyes, though Slade was a little darker. The three of us were all a year apart. Looking at our family, one would have a big question mark because Ansli and Yuri looked more like our friends than they did our family. They were mixed. Their biological mom was white, and their biological dad was black. They're my sisters because my parents adopted them. They were my dad's best friend's daughters, and he and his wife died in a plane crash when Ansli and Yuri were three and one years old, respectively. Ansli is only six months younger than me. I feel so sorry for her sometimes because she would just cry missing her parents even though mine had done a great job loving her and treating her no different than Slade or Sloan or me. She still has a hole in her heart.

"I'm serious, Dad. These candidates are toast," Sloan boasted.

My dad told her to shush as he looked around the room and looked over at the guy fiddling with the plates.

"Don't worry about him. He works here," I said to them, as I rolled my eyes at the help who'd come on strong when we were alone.

My mom said, "Stanley, you might as well fill them in on the candidates. This is going to be their first time being around them."

My dad had won a brutal primary election to become the Democratic nominee for the mayoral election coming up in November. Now, he had to go up against the Republican candidate, Willie Brown, who the papers have labeled a snake, and Avery James, an independent who was gaining lots of momentum because he was the only white candidate. My dad gave us the quick 411 on both of them.

Sloan asked, "Do you think Willie Brown is really a . . ."

"Somebody called my name! I heard my name called!" the loud-mouthed, obnoxious, light-skinned Mr. Brown uttered as he strolled into the room like he was king. I was puzzled as to why he went over to the waiter and brought him toward us. "You guys have met my son?"

"Stepson," the young guy blurted out.

"Son . . . stepson . . . don't correct me again," Mr. Brown harshly said to him. "So, Spencer, I sent you in here to spy. I'm sure this family the media portrays as so sweet has a bunch of issues. Tell me you got the dirt?"

My parents' eyebrows rose. Mr. Brown licked his lips like he had us. My sisters glared over at me like I was the bad guy who'd let in a snake. At that point, I felt sick. Feeling betrayed, I looked at the jerk and dashed out of the room, feeling completely humiliated.

***

I couldn't get into the bathroom fast enough. How dare that jerk play me like that? I couldn't remember what my family had said. I don't think there were any traded secrets or anything, but at the same time, I didn't want the opposition having any ammunition they could use against us. That was just sneaky, sly, and dead wrong. I was pacing back and forth so hard in this ladies' room, you would have thought I was trying to tread a hole in the tile.

"Not now, Ansli," I said as soon as my sister

followed me. "I'm not even trying to talk."

"Why are you getting mad at me? I'm just coming in here because Mom and Dad told me to come get you. You need to settle down. So what the hottie isn't who you thought he was? He's cute as he . . ."

"Okay, don't even go there," I said to her, knowing lately she's been a potty mouth.

"I'm just asking what's up with you, Shelby. You never let a guy get under your skin like that."

Pissed, I said, "I'm not used to being misled either."

"Did he tell you he was a waiter?"

Not wanting to answer, I slowly said, "No."

"Did you ask him if he was a waiter and he lied?"

"No."

Ansli threw up her hands in disgust and said, "Okay, so you just assumed, and since you assumed wrongly and he didn't correct you, you got a problem with the situation."

"He was being manipulative."

"We weren't even saying anything important. He was on the other side of the room stuffing his face with food when you thought he was bringing new food in. He got you. I think it's cute, charming, and what a fun way to start a relationship."

"Are you delusional? If I never see him again, it'll be too soon."

"You like him. I know you," she said in a coy voice.

"How can I like somebody I don't even know? I actually liked him better when I thought he was a waiter. I definitely don't like him now that I know he's the son . . ."

"*No, stepson,*" Ansli corrected me, acting silly.

"Ha-ha-ha, but exactly. Did you see how rude that Brown man was when he corrected him like that?"

"Yeah, they have a horrible relationship. I'm glad Dad doesn't treat me like a stepchild."

"Why do you keep saying that, Ansli? Dad loves you and Yuri just like he does me, Slade, and Sloan."

"I don't even want to argue with you," she said as she looked in the mirror, pulled out some makeup, and layered it on.

"You know Mom doesn't want you wearing it that thick."

"I'm lighter than you guys. I need more to look cute."

"That is such a crock. Don't put on all that. The last thing we need to do is get the folks all wound up at this debate."

"Really," she agreed, as she put it away.

"And have you seen that schedule we have to be on now that he's the true Democratic candidate? Almost every day we're going to be doing an appearance."

"We got to be like the Brady Bunch and stuff."

"Right," I agreed with my sister. "He is running for mayor. I didn't know *we* were running for mayor."

Ansli laughed and said, "Alright, well, I'm going to be out there. Hurry up in here."

"Can I go to the bathroom?" I said to her, tired of the short leash.

"Hey, don't shoot the messenger. I hope you don't have to do number two because we need you out there."

"Girl! That's TMI! Way too much information!"

"You said we're real sisters, right?"

"Oh, see . . . cute. Get out!"

Thankfully, I was feeling okay and didn't have to have an extended stay in the restroom. However, it was that time of the month. I did need to freshen myself.

I thought I came into the bathroom upset, but right after Ansli left, a lady wearing the cutest expensive heels came rushing in. She was crying. I didn't want to open the door because, clearly, she needed privacy. I mean, she could've looked under the stalls to see if she was alone, but she was, clearly, distraught.

I certainly didn't move when I heard her dial her phone and yell, "I can't take this anymore. If he hits me one more time, I might kill him!"

I knew I heard her right. I so wanted to leave the stall, hug her, and say, "Let's go to the nearest police station right now."

She continued, "I knew he was crazy before I married his tacky behind, but now I've got to go to appearances and act like everything is okay.

He put his hand on my face and arm. I didn't even say anything to set him off, and now we got this debate. I can't do it ... Wait, he's calling me now ... No, I'm not going to leave him. I love him."

Oh, you're a fool. I said to myself, as I listened in.

I searched in my purse to try to find my phone because I needed to text my sister to let her know what was up. Then I realized I left my phone in the greenroom. I wasn't trying to rush this lady or anything, but I really did need her to move on so I could move on. I mean I was sympathetic and all, but if she was saying she was still going to stay with the jerk who was hitting her, why should I worry?

Finally, when she left, I went to the sink, washed my hands, and rushed into the greenroom. As soon as I opened the greenroom door, those same striking shoes caught my eye. The lady who was just in the restroom crying her eyes out because she'd been beaten was the wife of the Republican candidate Willie Brown. She was Spencer's mom.

"Can we have some privacy, young lady?" Mr. Brown rudely said to me.

"This greenroom is for everybody," Spencer told him impudently.

Mr. Brown looked at Spencer like he wanted to sock him. Spencer glared back like "I dare you." I appreciated his spunk.

"I just came to get my phone," I said throwing my hand in the air.

I didn't need Spencer coming to my defense 'cause I didn't care what Mr. Brown thought. Now, I didn't just think he was a jerk because of his crude, obnoxious behavior. I knew he was an imbecile and certainly not someone who needed to be elected to run the city. I went over to where I'd been standing, and I didn't see my phone. Had my sister gotten it? Had someone else picked it up?

Spencer came over to me and touched my back. "I'm sorry about all that earlier."

I looked at him like, "Are you serious? Really?" I kept looking for my phone.

His stepdad was getting a little loud with his mom. He needed to be over there paying attention to that, but as soon as the door opened, I turned because I thought it was going to be my dad looking for me. Our family needed to stick together and keep up appearances. I was well aware of that, but I had to find my phone. The last thing I needed was for it to be in the wrong hands. It's not like it was a diary or anything, but with Instagram, Facebook, and Twitter, someone could hack into my account and copy a picture of me in a bathing suit from being at the beach last week and say I was a stripper or something.

Thankfully, my dad was not at the door. It was the independent candidate, Mr. James. Mr. Brown acted so nice with him. So fake and phony.

"Are you looking for this?" Spencer asked holding up my phone. "I shouldn't give it to you with you being mean to me and all."

As he dangled it in my face, I snatched it out of his hand and started walking out. The green-room was way too crowded. I wanted to be a part of the Brady Bunch rather than being in that stuffy room.

"Wait a minute, Shelby," Spencer said as he touched my arm real aggressively. "Why you keep running out on me?"

"Why do you insist on talking to me? Can't you read body language?" I jerked my hand away.

"Don't get mad. The polls have my step-dad leading, but that doesn't mean we can't be friends. I didn't even get a thank-you for finding your phone."

Going off, I said, "I didn't ask you to find it either."

"Come on. Don't be mad at me," he said as I continued to walk away. "We're not even old enough to vote. Or are you eighteen?"

"I'm so sick of the small talk, okay?"

I wanted so bad to tell him that if I were able to vote, there would be no way in the world I would vote for his stepdad. Hitting a woman? He would be the type to cheat on taxes, steal from the city, blackmail people, and hire his pitiful friends. As mad as I was that Mr. Brown was hitting his wife, there was no way I could tell Spencer—a guy I didn't like but who I barely knew—that his stepdad was a monster. However, Mr. Brown broke the silence when he came out of the greenroom, grabbing his wife by the front of her shirt.

"I can't believe you're letting your son talk to me like that. You better put that boy in check, or I will."

"Put me in check?" Spencer turned around and said. "I don't know who you think you're talking to, but you're not talking to my mom that way."

Because his back was turned, he didn't even see Mr. Brown handling his mom all crazy. Talking to her loud was only half the man's problem. I was fuming more than a race car getting revved up.

"Spencer, just calm down, Son," his mom came over and said to him.

Spencer uttered, "Nah, if he got something to say to me, just let him say it, and let me deal with this right now."

"You've been babying him for far too long. That's why he's always in trouble. You want him to come and live with us? Let me man him up,"

Mr. Brown spat.

I didn't even know Spencer, but I wanted to tell him, "Sock your stepdad in the jaw."

Spencer seemed to sense something wasn't right. "Let me talk to him, Mom. Back out of the way."

Mr. Brown pushed his wife out of the way and stepped closer to Spencer and said, "Yeah, move."

"Take your hands off my mom!" Spencer yelled.

"Where have you been? He obviously does that all the time," I blurted out.

Spencer whirled back at me. "What do you mean he does that all the time?"

Then I looked away, wishing I could take back the words, but really actually happy I said them. He needed to know, and it was the truth. I put my hands up in the air. I guess because we were getting louder in the hallway, people backstage started to crowd around.

"Shh, shh, shh," Mr. Brown started to say to his wife and stepson. "We can talk about this at home. Cameras are coming. Cut it out."

"Don't tell me to cut it out." Spencer looked at his mother. "Mom, has he been hitting you? Has he hurt you?"

She couldn't answer. She just looked away, but I glared at her arm. Hopefully, he was getting the hint. It was August, and she had on a long shirt. Spencer pushed up the fabric, and when he saw the deep bruise, he was livid. He quickly grabbed Mr. Brown's collar and pushed him toward the stage.

"I can't believe what you started!" his mother looked at me and yelled.

I would never disrespect an older woman. My mom taught me way better than that, but how dare she get mad at me because her son was defending her against a fool. So I just gave her a silly "I'm-sorry-that-you're-mad" kind of look, but I truly hoped that her husband got his butt kicked.

"You just want to embarrass my husband so he gets out of this election. This is all a ploy."

"You think this is about the election?" I finally spoke up and shouted. "I feel bad for you."

The tussling came back toward the greenroom. Mr. Brown passed his wife and yelled, "You need to get him off of me! He's ruining everything."

His wife appeared frantic. Mr. Brown had no problem hitting her, but he was whining when a guy pinned him up. Spencer was getting some great blows in. Security ended up pulling them apart.

"I can't go out there looking like this," Mr. Brown yelled. "Handle him."

Security reacted and got real rough with Spencer. I tried to step in, but my dad stepped right in the way.

"Where do you think you're going? The debate is canceled. They told everyone one of us got sick. We're going home, and now that I see what's the real deal, you're not following some thug."

"But, Dad, you don't understand. You don't know what happened," I said, needing to follow Spencer and the security.

"Yeah. I don't understand what happened either," the independent candidate came over and said. "I was ready to take on you guys today."

"I don't know if I could say I was ready," my dad humbly replied back. "But I guess it's going to have to hold off now. See you later, Mr. James."

Mr. James waved, shook his head at Spencer, and left with his entourage.

"What were you doing over there with that young man?" my mom came up behind me and asked. "And now he's fighting? That's horrible."

"Mom, you don't even know the whole story."

I tried walking away, but she snatched me back real quick.

"You come back here. We're going straight to the car now. There're too many reporters around here, and we're not trying to have any crazy incident like those guys just had."

"In a second I'll go straight to the car, Mom. I'm not going to embarrass you, but you don't know what's going on."

I wanted to yell, "You got to let him go! You got to let him go!" When I got to the back door, I heard Mr. Brown say to his wife, "It's him or me." She just looked at her son like "What am

I supposed to do?" As the security roughly car-
ried Spencer away, all I could do was feel sorry
for the stranger.

CHAPTER TWO
STORY

"Shelby Grace, I said I'm not trying to hear it. Get in the limousine! You see all these reporters out there?" my dad said to me in the angriest voice I'd ever heard him use toward me.

"Stanley, you need to calm down," my mom leaned over and whispered to him. "There's already been one candidate that couldn't control himself tonight. Let's not make it two."

My dad gave Mom a look as if she'd let him down.

The driver held the limo door open, and I dared not to get in. I could tell my father wasn't finished talking to me, so I let my sisters pass by. Yuri, Slade, and Sloan all looked at me as if I let them down too. I really had a tight bond with Ansli ... maybe because we were in the same grade, but imagine your best friend actually being your sister and being able to come home with her each night. It was special because I didn't have to hold things back from her. I could get her straight when she needed it, and she didn't have a problem telling me what she felt either.

Ansli pushed me into the limousine and said into my ear, "You sit far away from Mom and Dad. Don't give him any ammunition to stay mad, and don't try to tell him what happened while we are in the car. Wait until we get home."

"What happened, Dad? Why didn't we have the debate?" inquisitive Sloan asked.

Everybody eyed her down.

"Oh, I'm not supposed to ask that?" Sloan annoyingly blurted out.

"How many more of these things are we going to have to go to?" shy Yuri asked.

"As many of them as your father needs,"

my mom answered, even though the question wasn't directed toward her. "Seriously, Stanley, you need to calm down," she said, sensing my father was still upset because he wouldn't even look at us. He loved looking at his girls, telling us how proud of us he is.

Instead, he groaned, "You girls just whine all the time. It's like you don't appreciate anything. The reporters are asking tons of questions. I got a text from Lou. He's going to meet us at the house."

My dad's campaign manager was a pain in the butt. He kept pushing us to appear perfect. I knew they had a strategy and wanted to win, but we could only be who we were. My dad was disappointed in me. I could feel it.

Finally, when the tension was so thick in the limo that you couldn't even chop it with an ax, I said, "Dad, I'm sorry if I let you down. I was just trying to tell you . . ."

He cut me off and said, "Didn't I tell you, Shelby, that I didn't want to know any particulars about that family? I'm running a clean race. You're always trying to fix things. Why can't you just stay in your lane and take care of Shelby?"

"You don't need to be so harsh with her?" My mom stepped up.

"Whose side are you on?" Dad shot back.

"Our family's side."

"Well, you were just saying backstage how you were disappointed that she was inserting herself into someone else's life," my father reminded her.

"Yes, but we can talk to her off-line about whatever any of our girls want to discuss. I don't like the loud tone you're using," my mother said.

My dad looked up and saw ten eyes glaring back at him. "So you're going to correct me in front of the girls? Just great."

"We can just agree to disagree," my mother said as she sat back and motioned for us all to look away. We saw her grab his hand. "I still love ya though."

When she saw my dad pull his hand away, Slade, never wanting any conflict, uttered "Great, now you've got our parents mad at each other."

I didn't want any conflict either. My mom's body stiffened, and I could tell that she was not happy with him. My dad wasn't happy with her either. He said so and kept staring out the window. But I did appreciate that, though they argued, as I'm sure all parents do at some point, there was no threat of blooming violence. My mother was safe to have her own opinion. While I hated that I was the cause of any kind of tension, I knew we'd be alright. I could only hope and pray things were better for Spencer.

"I'm sorry, girls," my dad said, finally giving in and making my mom beam with pride that he listened. "I am proud of you all. I know you know how to handle yourselves. I'm just getting more texts from Lou. He's already at the house, and there's a swarm of reporters waiting on us."

We lived in an upscale neighborhood with a guard gate. However, since some homeowners had not paid their fee, the gate was unattended because the complex couldn't afford to pay an attendant. It's been open for the last few months, and people were able to come and go as they pleased.

"A bunch of reporters? Honey, I don't want the girls photographed all over the place," my mom said.

"I hate that we aren't in our car. We could've driven right into the garage and closed it," my dad said, wanting to protect us. "Don't feel like you have to answer any questions."

When the driver came around and opened the door for us, pandemonium erupted. Lights flashed, cameras were snapped, and mics were in our faces. With the way the media was treating us, you would have thought my dad was actually president of the United States.

A fat, sweaty reporter stepped too close and blabbed, "Girls, I heard you were going to public school this year. That's going to be a big switch from private school."

Though we've been told not to respond, I think all of us said, "No, we're not."

My mother quickly escorted us inside. All of us were pacing back and forth. We needed to talk to my dad. We needed answers. No way in the world were we planning to go to public school. What in the world was that announcement all about? And as soon as he came in the door, we started drilling him.

"Okay, girls. Just settle down. I'm just saying public school helped me start from the bottom and get here," he started trying to talk all young, hip, and cool to us. "I didn't grow up privileged. I built my law practice from the ground up. I got to the NFL because I worked hard and went for what I wanted at a young age. You girls have had a silver spoon in your mouth all your life, and it's time you start learning you can't just hold your hand out and want us to give you things. You've got to start making your own way."

"But why do we have to go to public school to learn that lesson?" I said.

Sloan asked, "Yeah, Dad, is this for you or for us?"

He looked appalled. Sloan stepped back, realizing she'd said too much. Lots of thoughts were wrestling around in my head about why for us going to public school is a bad idea, but none of it mattered. My dad had made up his mind, my mom supported his decision, and that was the end of the story. We were going to take it, deal with it, and make it work. It just seemed so unfair and it seemed like such a political move, but that didn't matter.

***

"Shelby! Get up!" my sister Sloan jabbed me in the ribs and said. "We're not sleeping in today. We're getting up and fixing Mom and Dad breakfast. We are not going to public school."

I pulled the covers over my head. I wasn't even thinking about my younger sisters. Yuri was shy, so she wasn't saying anything. Slade wanted to be famous so she wasn't trying to upset Dad because anywhere where the cameras were, that's where she wanted to be. If she thought cameras were going to be in public school, she was down with that plan. However, Sloan was very outspoken, the community activist of our family, and because she thought our rights were being violated and we weren't going to have the best education that our parents could afford for us, she felt that they needed to change their minds.

"Come on, Shelby! Seriously!" Sloan said as she snatched the covers off my face.

"Seriously, you need to leave me alone," I said in a tough voice. I knew she loved having her way, but when I put my foot down, she didn't try me. I wanted to go back to sleep, so I turned over.

I could hear Sloan mumbling to Slade and Yuri. Then Yuri coughed and said, "Fixing breakfast for them would be nice, Shelby. We just need your help. You're the one who cooks the best."

I rolled back over and eyed her. "Yuri, are you serious? You're the best cook in the house."

"Yeah, you are, Yuri," Slade agreed, wondering why Yuri would make such a dumb comment to convince me.

"That's just because I spend a lot of time with the cooks Mom and Dad hired, but you make the best homemade pancakes because you got the recipe from Grandma," Yuri said, making a great point.

"Just please get up. We're going to be going to school soon. We need to spend time together," Slade said. "Plus, you heard Dad's campaign manager. We've got to be more of a tight unit."

I stood up. "What do you want us all to do? Dress alike and follow in line behind each other?"

"Whatever it's going to take to help Dad win, we should be down for it."

"No, speak for yourself," Slade said, and then the two of them started going at it.

"Where's Ansli?" I asked.

Sloan said, "We came and got you first. We know you can get Ansli up."

"Alright. I'll meet y'all in the kitchen."

I knew there was more to Ansli not being as social than they understood. She was a morning person. She'd always been the one coming into my room, jumping on me, and trying to get me up and stuff. She actually hated that we didn't share a room anymore. Though we were best buddies and loved each other as sisters, I did want my space, but it was killing her. Most of the nights, she'd end up in my room anyway. So for her not to bother me meant something was up.

Then it dawned on me. It's August. The anniversary of her parents' death. While the details were vague to us because our parents wanted to shield us all from the tragedy, every year around this time, she retreated. I needed to pull her out of her gloom. The good thing about it was she and I shared a bathroom between our rooms. She loved locking out our younger sisters by her bedroom door, but she never locked me out, and the bathroom door was never shut either. This time it was.

"Ansli, you in there?" I said, not wanting to just bulldoze my way in.

"I'm not feeling that good, Shelby. We can talk later, alright? I heard they want y'all to make them breakfast. Go do that. Go make your parents something to eat."

Okay, see now I was mad. I knew what she was going through, so I couldn't let her know I was mad, but these weren't just my parents. My parents adopted her, and she had our last name. Why was she trippin'? I couldn't even imagine what she was going through. Not only did she and Yuri not look like my parents, but just knowing that she'd never see her biological folks again had to hurt bad. However, my folks had given her all they had, and she had a lot of life to live. Someway, somehow, she was going to have to embrace her pain and become stronger from it. As her sister and her friend, it was my job to make sure that happened. So I just opened the door and jumped into her bed like she usually jumped into mine.

"Okay, what's this?"

"Well, you can't kick me out because you do this to me all the time."

"I know, but I'm tired, and when you tell me you're tired, I leave you alone, right?"

"No, so don't even try it! What's wrong?" I said, as I stroked her beautiful, naturally curly hair. Being mixed did have its privileges. Not only did she have a gorgeous, golden skin tone, but her hair was prettier than Indian hair.

"I know you miss your parents. I'm sorry."

"You can't begin to know how this feels."

"And I'm not trying to. I guess I'm just saying my folks, our folks, love you too. So let's cook them breakfast. You don't want to go to public school any more than I do. So we got to talk them out of this craziness. Right? Let's join as sisters and make sure we're straight. Come on! Come on!" I said, tickling her and knowing that that always worked.

Sure enough, she started smiling. I knew it wasn't a real smile. I knew deep down she was still hurting. When she got up, I said, "We're older now. Me and you can talk to Mom and try to get more details about your parents if that's what you want."

"You'd want to know?"

"Yeah, if you want to know, I want to know."

"And you think she'd tell me?" Ansli asked.

"I do. I think she'll tell you. I think she'd tell you anything you want to know."

"Thank you, Shelby." She hugged me.

About an hour later, we were waking our parents up. I couldn't believe it was just six thirty in the morning, but we were trying to show them that we needed them to hear us out.

"Okay, so what do you guys want? I know it's something," my dad said. "We're not getting all this love, breakfast, and attention just because you guys want to be sweet daughters."

Nobody said anything, and this was Sloan's idea, but she looked at me.

So I uttered, "Dad, we're just not trying to do the whole public . . ."

"Don't even go there, Shelby. You guys are going to public school."

Then we all started whining at once.

He said, "I'm serious. I told you guys last night. You got to get in there and understand the real world. We sheltered you way too long."

"Dad, is that really what all of this is about?" Sloan asked. "Don't you think you want to send us there because you'll get better mileage for your campaign if that's where we go?"

Handing us back the plate, he said, "No, I think I'll get better daughters, and because you guys would even insinuate that, it goes to show that I'm making the right decision. Your mom and I talked about it. We appreciate the breakfast, but next week, you're going to school where we say you're going to school. That's all. You aren't any better than anyone else, and I think public school will humble you a little bit."

At that time, all five of us tried to plead, but

Mom cut us off. She said, "Girls, we've already decided. End of story. Deal with it."

***

Slade was the first one at the car ready to go to the debate. The media wasted no time rescheduling the one that got canceled a couple of days before. There was tons of speculation as to why the debate was abruptly called off, and no one was buying the story that one of the candidates became ill. I knew the real reason, and driving over there, though I was supposed to be listening to Lou give us a briefing that would help us answer any questions that came our way, the only thing I could think about was Spencer.

This debate wasn't in the nicest part of town. Actually, it was in the hood. While I was sure every public school didn't look like the one we were in, this one certainly needed renovating. The grass wasn't cut, bars were on some windows, inside it looked like the place need to be painted, and so much graffiti was on the walls. We just looked at my dad like, "Is this where you plan to send us?"

Frustrated, he said, "Guys, your public school isn't even zoned for over here. Just let me get through this debate. Go sit with your mom."

I was following the crowd. I wanted to go backstage, see if I could find Spencer, talk to him, and make sure he was okay. However, because I had to be with my mom and because of what happened last time, families weren't allowed backstage, and at this school, it didn't seem like there was a backstage anyway.

"You're preoccupied," Ansli gave me a hip bump and declared.

It was no use for me to try to hide what was going on from her. She knew me from the inside out. I was so happy that she was out of her pity-partying state.

"You've been smiling a lot and on that phone a lot. Is it someone new I need to know about?" I asked her.

"It's this Hispanic guy on Instagram. I commented on his pictures."

"He's not half nude or anything is he?"

Frowning at me, Ansli said, "No, he draws. I comment on the pictures that he draws."

Smiling, I uttered, "Oh. He's an artist. Like you."

"We've just been talking back and forth. I don't know. Talking to Hugo is not a big deal or anything."

"Hugo? Go ahead, senorita," I said as I bumped her back. "Do you know if he is who he says he is though? It's harder to talk online to someone you've never met. It just seems a little weird to me."

"That's why I didn't want to tell you about him," Ansli was angry. "You know what? Forget it."

"No, no, I'm just making sure you're okay."

"Whatever, Shelby. You been going crazy over a guy you just saw one time. At least I've been talking back and forth with this guy."

"I'm not going crazy over a guy I only met once."

"So you're not sitting here trying to figure out where the dude is from the other day? You're not looking around here trying to make sure he's alright? You aren't hoping you run into him?"

"NO!"

"You're lying."

"Okay, I'm lying, but it's not because I like him. I only want to make sure he's alright."

"Please. Save the lies for the spies. I'm your girl. I'm on your side. You don't have to front with me."

"And don't go telling them about . . ."

Ansli said, "Like I would ever tell any of our sisters anything. You don't trust them either."

"Tell us what?" Sloan, one of the three musketeers, shocked us and said.

I got her straight. "Sloan, no one was even talking about y'all or to y'all."

"Whatever, Shelby. Something's going on between you two."

"Good point. Something's going on between the two of us, not between the three of us," I teased, but she didn't laugh. I softened, "Come on. Let's go sit down. The debate is about to start."

We sat down just as the curtain pulled back. The room was packed. The local CBS news affiliate reporter Sandra Lemons, whom

I admired because of her spunk, introduced all three candidates. "Let's give it up for Mr. Avery James, the independent candidate; Vice President of First Charlotte Bank Mr. Willie Brown, the Republican candidate; and attorney Stanley Sharp, the Democratic nominee."

The debate was going on and on. I'm not saying it was boring, but how many ways could three different people say the same thing? They all wanted to save the city from crime, to increase the revenue, and to improve education. Not that those weren't noble things, but it just wasn't something a teen was interested in. Maybe I should be, but I wasn't.

"Mom, I gotta go to the restroom," I leaned over and said.

"Be quick about it, Shelby. You should've taken care of all that before the debate started."

"I mean, I can wait, but I'm just trying to go before the debate is over and everyone has to go. Or before Dad's ready to go and I haven't gone."

"Girl . . . go," my mom said to me.

As soon as I got to the ladies' room, I didn't have to go anymore because there was Spencer's mom fiddling with her neckline, trying to cover something up. Had Mr. Brown choked her? As soon as the door closed, she jumped. I could see what she was covering with her hand, and it was another bruise.

"Oh, my gosh, I'm so embarrassed," she said, realizing who I was.

I had on one of my scarts, so I immediately took it off and said, "Here. Use this."

It wasn't my place to ask her why she was enduring torture, but it was in my heart to help. Her eyes were red and watery, and like a statue, she just stood there and let me fix her up. I turned her toward the mirror, and a few tears dropped.

"This is beautiful. Where did you get this?" she asked.

"I made it."

The melon-colored scart looked great on her black dress. It actually made it pop. I thought I saw a smile.

"It can be a belt too," I said as I showed her how the silk material would zip into her lap and create a whole different, cool look.

"Can we please keep this between us?"

"Yes. Yes, ma'am," I said, assuring her. "I won't say a word."

"Thank you. I know I was rude to you last time I saw you, and I'm sorry. There's a lot going on right now, but you know...your dad's a candidate. Campaigns make people crazy. There's a lot going on in my family, you know?"

She was trying to rationalize it since I was just a teenager. She could tell me anything, and I could act like I believed it, but I did want to know about Spencer. I couldn't explain why, but I couldn't let her walk away without me asking where he was.

"And your son?" I said before she hit the door. "He didn't like go to jail or anything?"

She sighed, "No, honey. He's living with his father now, and I know he thinks living with his father is like being in jail. But I had no choice. Spencer and my husband don't get along. I'm not trying to punish him, but I can't let him mess up what I built. I don't even know why I shared all of this, but don't worry about Spencer. He's okay, and if you never see him again, your life will be much better. He's my son, and I love him, but he is a handful."

"You're looking at me like you're disappointed," Mrs. Brown shared, noticing the frown that I didn't realize was forming on my face as I heard her tell the story.

CHAPTER THREE
SOPHISTICATED

A couple of days later, all seemed right with the world. My dad was ahead in the polls. We'd been to open house at our new school, and it was actually a brand-new public school. Though I would only be there for one year, my graduating class would be the first. Lots of people were being transferred from other schools due to overcrowding. Everybody in town wanted to attend Marks High School, and though it wasn't far from where we lived, I didn't think this was the school we were zoned for. But my dad did have pull, and as long as I had the right attitude, maybe this could be a great year after all.

As soon as we stepped in the school doors, my sister Ansli was smiling wider than I was. "Yes, yes," she groaned.

"Okay, so what's going on with you?"

"I've been dying to tell you," Ansli leaned in and said.

"Don't shout it!" I told her, as our three younger sisters followed behind the two of us.

I'm sure we looked like we were a sorority. Matching blazers with an *S* on them, cool plaid skirts that weren't too short but definitely not too long, and white button-down shirts with different colored scarts that I tied in various ways to match our personalities. My dad wanted us to represent. Slade wanted to get us noticed. Yuri didn't care. Sloan wanted somebody to comment, and Ansli . . . yeah, I had to figure out why she was so giddy. Her personality ebbed and flowed more than a river.

"What is going on with you? Why are you so happy?" I asked.

"Hugo goes to this school."

My eyes widened. "Are you sure? You haven't met him yet."

"He told me he goes here, and I've seen his pictures."

"How do you know that's even him? You know people lie about that stuff nowadays."

"Why you tryna deflate my hopes? I've got a great feeling about this guy. He's not lying to me."

"I'm sure the Hispanic sisters are not going to be happy with him falling all over you."

"We actually talked about that. I was a little insecure with it at first," she said.

Ansli was insecure about everything. She always needed somebody to reassure her that she was on point. But I just didn't want this guy to crush her since she was putting all her excitement in this relationship working out.

Girls could, for sure, be cruel. Even in our previous small, little isolated private school of about a hundred students, the Sharp sisters had haters. So I knew with over three thousand students roaming around at Marks High that we were going to have issues. We were cute, smart girls who came from a highly popular family. And while I was not trying to apologize for who we were, I wasn't trying to be punked nor did I want any of my sisters to bring unnecessary attention to us. Having my biracial sister dating a Hispanic guy was certainly going to draw some attention.

"He said he was tired of the Latino girls. He said that they were fake and tried to act classy but were just as ghetto as could be."

That seemed so funny. But I didn't really spend time with a lot of Latino girls, so I didn't know if that was true or not. I sure knew a bunch of black girls were ghetto, and that's why going to a public school where they were the majority was not something I was fully sold on.

"Wait! There he is."

When she grabbed my arm, the five of us stopped walking, and the Hispanic hottie walked our way. I took a gulp. I could see why she was into him.

Ansli was salivating. "He looks better in person. Oh my gosh!"

"Who looks better in person?" Sloan said, like she was some kind of reporter.

I mean that girl never missed anything.

"Y'all need to go to class."

"Yeah, but you need to go to the mall. Didn't you get the memo? We don't wear uniforms at this school," a smarty-pants wench said.

Ansli looked at me like her eyes were begging me to get everyone out of her way.

"Come on, y'all, let's get to class," I said, as I reached back and pulled one of my sisters right through the snobby girl standing in our way.

Like I cared what she thought about our dress. Her style was so tacky; the last thing she needed to be doing was trying to talk about us. And the little goons with her seemed like they couldn't even think for themselves. They were laughing at her stupid remark, but when I glared at all of them and left them standing there like her words didn't faze me, they all seemed pissed. Seeing their displeasure made me happy.

"I'm glad we already registered and got our classes at open house. Look at that line of new students," Sloan said.

And as soon as I glanced over there, I did a double take because I thought I saw Spencer. I had to talk to him. I had to find him. I had to apologize, but Yuri said she couldn't find her class. When I pointed her in the direction of D hall, she finally felt like she could make it on her own, so I went back toward the registration line and realized the guy I saw wasn't Spencer at all. It was only me wishing it was him.

"Now, there're some sharp girls!" Principal Garner said to us. "I wanted my kids to come in here in uniforms. I should have known Stanley's girls would set the best example. You all look so adorable."

Now, I was starting to think maybe this wasn't a great idea. I had done some work on the blazers my mom picked up for us, added some rhinestones and some ribbon, and took them in a couple of places to add some pleats. I wanted to show off our style. I didn't want an adult to think it was cool. I waved bye to my sisters, but the principal didn't go anywhere.

"I'm going to be late, Dr. Garner," I said, not wanting any special favors or anyone thinking that the mayoral candidate's daughter had the principal on lock. But he wouldn't move.

"Sir, I got to get to class."

"I know. I just wanted to tell you your dad just called to make sure you girls were okay, so I'd been walking around school trying to find you."

Livid, I said, "My dad called you?"

"Oh, it's no big deal. I told him I'd keep an eye out. It's a new school and all. Truth be told, he helped me get the job."

That was just great. My dad was always pulling strings. Now, the man felt he owed him.

"We've got a hodgepodge of everybody in this school, but I know you're going to be a leader. You're a senior. Your dad tells me you're a bright girl, Miss Shelby. I've got to learn all your sisters' names, but at least I know you. We'll be having an election soon for the student government association. Since it's a new school, nobody could run last year, so I expect you to run for president. Put us on the map in a grand fashion."

"I'm not interested in that, sir. Politics is my father's thing."

"Come on, be well rounded. I'll put your name down. Nobody will probably run against a Sharp anyway. Well, except, I hear we've got Mr. Brown's stepson coming to this school."

I wasn't listening to Dr. Garner, but then I tuned in. "What? Who?"

"Nothing, don't worry about him."

"Okay, I have to get to class." And I had pep in my step. I did see Spencer. Wow, maybe Ansli wasn't the only one who was going to like being a Marks Maverick.

***

So it was lunchtime, and at a big school, I didn't have a lunch period with any of my sisters. I hadn't seen Spencer, and I hadn't made any friends. Good thing about all of that is that I didn't always have to be with somebody, probably because I came from a big family. Anytime I had alone time was a good time. This school had everything on the menu: a pizza bar, a salad bar, hot foods, and snacks. When I saw the Chick-fil-A stand, I dashed toward it. A chicken sandwich with waffle fries and a shake had my name all over it.

"I'm surprised you're eating fast food. You're

one of them uppity girls," this scruffy, deep-voiced guy huffed.

I didn't even look up because I didn't ask him for his opinion, and I wasn't trying to entertain him or talk to him more.

"Oh, you *are* one of those stuck-up girls. But I like them kind. Y'all sit down," he said to the other guys with him.

A whole bunch of guys wearing maroon and gray T-shirts with a big football on them put their trays down around me. Inwardly, I was thinking I should have sat alone at a table with some nerds or something because at least if they bothered me, it would be an intelligent conversation. These flunkies looked like they didn't know their left from their right. Since they were a part of the team and had probably been at school in the summer, maybe the table was theirs. So I started getting up. But the deep-voiced guy, who seemed to be the captain, firm-ly put his hands around my wrist and pulled me back down.

"Naw, naw, sit. I'm Fritz. This is Poncho, Joey, and Phil. We don't want a pretty girl like you sitting all alone."

Needing an excuse to tip away, I uttered, "It's okay. It's the first day of school. Like most people, I'm new here. I don't know anybody but my sisters."

"They them daughters of that man running for mayor," the stocky Joey guy uttered.

"I'm Shelby," I said confirming my own identity.

Fritz sucked his teeth and said, "You looking good in that skirt. I saw you prancing around here with your head all up high. They already had cheerleading tryouts, but I could get you on if you want. The way you working that booty, I can tell you . . ."

Cutting him off, I huffed, "Okay, okay, you don't know me like that to be talking like that."

"I didn't mean to offend you, dang. How a brother supposed to talk to you? You don't like white boys and crap, do you? There's some around here to choose from, but um, being with da brothers is where it's at, my sister."

I wasn't trying to be with no ignorant guy,

so I got up again. "Y'all can have this table."

Fritz shouted, "I said I don't need you to go nowhere."

"You don't tell me what I am supposed to do!"

His partner Joey said, "Ooh."

I suppose he wasn't used to a female talking to him like that because he stood up and towered over me. "You ain't got to front on me in front of all these people."

But then a guy stood between us. "And you ain't got to put your funky breath up in a girl's face."

The guy pushed Fritz back some. I looked up and was stunned to see Spencer. Not that I needed him to rescue me, but if that's what it took for him to cross my path again, I was grateful.

"Wait, dude, you better watch it!" Fritz got buck and said.

"Uh! It's alright, Fritz. He didn't mean nothing by it," I said just trying to calm the guy down. "I guess I do know somebody else here. He's my cousin."

Fritz eyed Spencer down. "Well, you better tell your cousin to chill."

I grabbed my tray, pushed Spencer in the back, and we went to some tables outside.

"I'm your cousin now?" he laughed.

"I had to calm the guy down with something, but you didn't have to jump in. I had it."

"It didn't look like you had it from where I was sitting."

"So you were watching me?" I said to him.

He looked away.

"Not big, bad Spencer. I know you're not shy."

"A lot's been going on, that's all," he voiced.

And when he said that, it took me back to the seriousness of all that had been going on with him. Last time I saw him he was being carted out of a room. I knew he had a temper, and I certainly didn't want him getting in trouble in school over me. But I did want to ask the tough questions. I wanted to get to know him. I wanted to find out where he'd been. At least I knew he was okay, but was he really okay?

"I've been worried about you," I said. "And

I owe you a big apology. I've been dreaming about . . ."

"Wait, you talking about me watching you . . . you've been dreaming about me?"

"No, forget I said that." But he was beaming, totally happy I was into him. Though I had caramel skin, I'm sure my cheeks were rosy red from blushing. "I saw your mom the other day. She told me you were living with your dad. Are you okay with all that?"

Getting agitated, he said, "I really don't want to talk about it, Shelby."

In a softer tone, I uttered, "I'm sorry. I'm not trying to get in your business, but I do feel responsible."

"But you're not the one who hit my mom. You didn't make her decide to keep enduring that over supporting her own son. My dad's an alcoholic and a gambler. He's always had a little temper. My mom got out of a marriage with him and got into a marriage with someone equally foul. And she feels that just because Mr. Brown can provide her with the lifestyle she's used to, she can look over the wrong that he does."

"But if I wouldn't have said anything . . ."

"I sort of knew. I looked the other way because my mom wanted me to look the other way. She brought me to live with them because she was scared of him. She won't admit it, but I'm not stupid. She wants me to act a certain way and pretend like I'm okay with her getting knocked around occasionally."

"I'm sorry you had to move away from your mom to live with your dad."

"He's not that bad anymore. Besides, I'm a senior this year. I'm really in both of their ways. Pretty soon I'll be on my own, so whatever. I'll see you around," Spencer said before getting up.

Something I said didn't sit well with him. We were having a simple conversation, and then he was gone. I guess I pried too much. Watching him walk away I was impressed. Everything on his backside made me smile.

"Dang, your cousin's fine," an irritating voice from earlier interrupted me from taking in the sight that was fading away.

I looked up and confirmed it was the girl who tried to front on my clothes.

"I'm Lyrica. I was trying to talk to you this morning."

"No, you were trying to go off on me this morning."

"Well, let me just set a few ground rules since you're new here."

"This is a new school. Last time I checked I think we're all new here."

"No, most of us came from Robert E. Lee High School. A few of you guys are new. The guys you were talking to over there, well, the cutie-pie is mine. Fritz Black. Don't even think about trying to get with him."

"Telling me who you think I can't have . . . ," I said as I stood up and eyed this Lyrica chick down, ". . . is the wrong thing. Your guy was after me."

"You don't want to cross me," she said, thinking I would flinch.

I picked up my tray, crossed right in front of her, and said, "I think I just did." I left her standing there to figure it all out . . . like I was scared of her behind, whatever.

"Oh no, you didn't!" Lyrica yelled really

loudly as I heard her coming toward me.

"You need to step back, missy," a soft but high-pitched male voice said.

So I turned around. Was somebody defending me? And there stood the most stylish, coolest character I'd seen at the school. It was a guy with turquoise pants on and with a two-toned fro sprayed pink and gold that formed a *V* in the back. He had on yellow, wide-rimmed glasses with no lenses in the frames. He was sporting a blinged-out belt. The way his hand was on his hip and the fact that he had on girl's tennis shoes, I knew this dude wasn't a typical guy.

"Jay, move out the way," Lyrica told him like she knew him—with attitude, clearly not caring for him.

"It's Jazzy Jay, baby, and *you* get to stepping. We don't want a repeat of the incident we had last year. You got embarrassed so bad you tee-teed on yourself."

"Whatever, Jay," Lyrica said, as she flicked her hand.

"*Jazzy Jay*, baby, but you wouldn't know anything about jazzy now would you?" he said, checking her out like she was a welfare case.

Lyrica looked my way and said, "Scrub, Ms. Jazzy got your back and stuff, but you better watch it."

"Do I look scared?" I quickly told her.

"Boo!" Jazzy Jay jumped and said, making Lyrica jump and pitifully hip-hop away like a one-legged rabbit.

We both started cracking up when she high-tailed it away.

"I'm Shelby, Jazzy Jay." Clearly I heard his name.

He smiled. "You are sassy, Shelby. I like you're style, girl. I had a class with your sistah Miss Ansli, and she told me how you hooked up her jacket. I was going to take it off of her, but she said you'd kill her. I've been looking for you for three periods. Tell the truth. How is my attire?"

"Honest?"

"That's the only way I like it! She said you're a real fashionista, and I can see that. My cousin is a designer, and I'm trying to get her to let me work with her, but she says I need to up my game and be a little more original. So, what ya think?"

"You put it together well, but is any of it yours?"

"Oh, you crush!"

"I better get to government. It was nice meeting you, Jazzy."

"Hold up now! That's where I'm going. Mr. Freeman's class?"

I nodded when I looked at my schedule and saw I had Mr. Freeman. Jazzy was popular with everybody. Everywhere we went people were giving him high fives, giving him shout-outs, and asking him about their outfits.

"Thanks for stepping in with Lyrica back there," I told him as we walked to class.

"Uh, Ms. Goody Two-shoes thinks she owns the world. Fronting like her family got loot . . . she don't even have two nickels to rub together. I heard she on free and reduced lunch just like me."

"Well, if she knew what I know, that's not a bad thing."

"You know a rich girl would say that."

"I'm not rich. My dad makes it clear that his

and my mom's money is not my and my sisters' money."

"Yeah, but every time you got your hand out, they fill it, don't they?"

"Not really."

"Well, if your parents work hard and got it for you, don't be ashamed of that. Poor people in the mess we in because our parents made piss-poor choices. Everybody could have got up off their tail and done betta. I was born black and gay, and that ain't gonna change. I was born poor and born into the wrong body, and I'm working on both."

"Oh, you are silly!"

"Just real, Miss Shelby, just real."

"You want to be a girl?"

"Naw, I like who I am, but a little tits and tail ain't never hurt nobody," he said as he swatted me on the behind.

"Ouch!"

"Don't act like you don't like it!"

"Should I be worried?" I said, looking at him until we walked into Mr. Freeman's room. Both of us froze goo-goo eying over Spencer.

"I saw him first!" Jazzy Jay said.

"Hey, Shelby, come sit by me," Spencer invited.

"Dang, looks like he ain't even interested. Handle that, girl, for the both of us."

"You are stupid," I turned and jokingly said to my new friend.

"So, you're not mad at me anymore, huh?" I asked Spencer when I sat down beside him.

"I had no right to get upset with you."

"I'm Jazzy Jay, and you would be?"

"Spencer, what's up?"

"What's up?" Jazzy Jay said with awe. "The muscles you are flexing on your chest are what's up."

"Alright everybody sit down. I'm Mr. Freeman. I hear everybody's been a little wild today. I know you guys are seniors and think you run the school. It's a new school, but I got new house rules in here. We can have fun, but we're gonna get a lesson. I run the show!" Mr. Freeman called roll, and he seemed impressed when he found out who I was.

"You guys know her dad's running for mayor

and everything?"

And I wanted to say, "And so is his stepdad."

But Spencer looked at me like, "Don't you even open your mouth!" And I could understand. I wouldn't want to claim Willie Brown either.

"I'm just a student."

"Now, you are, but when your dad wins, you're going to be one of the first kids of the city. I know you're going to do well in here . . . ," Mr. Freeman leaned in and uttered, "the mayor's daughter and all."

"Sir, my dad hasn't won, and he doesn't like us to speak as though he has. Trust me, there are some candidates out there who, even though he's up in the polls today, are trying to make sure that my dad doesn't win."

"Well, that's a very first-class response. You know what, I need to talk to you anyway. Alright guys, turn to page 6 and start reading chapter 1. Do the discussion questions at the end."

Mr. Freeman came right over to me and said, "I'm just going to keep it real. I want to be

in politics. I just got this job because I was trying to work for the city, but nothing was avail-
able. I had the credentials, and the school system was looking for male teachers. I know your
dad hasn't chosen everybody who's going to
serve in his administration. I wanted to know if
I get you a résumé, would you show it to him? Is
there somebody I need to call? You know, what's
the heads-up?"

"I don't know, sir, but I could find out and
tell you."

"Oh, that'd be great! And don't worry about
your grade; I got you. At least this semester, because when he wins, I'm out!"

"Like he wants your brownnosing butt
around," Jazzy Jay said after Freeman walked
away.

"Oh, so you were listening?"

"Of course I was listening."

"I heard it too," Spencer said. "You know,
you're probably going to get a lot of that cuz
you looked all shocked, like you couldn't believe he was trying to get stuff out of you
because of who you are. It's been happening

to me a lot."

"Why has it been happening to you? You ain't no Sharp. I mean, you're sharp but..." Jazzy Jay said.

"I'm just saying," Spencer said to Jazzy, not wanting to reveal his identity.

Diverting the conversation, I jumped in. "I just can't believe him. He's my teacher, and of course I want to help him out. I don't want him to give me an F."

Spencer said, "Yeah, but what is it that you want out of life? As many people who are going to start coming at you for stuff because of who your dad is, start using them the same way."

"Oh yeah, that's wassup. She wants to be a fashion designer," Jazzy Jay added.

Spencer nodded. "I'm sure there are people in this city who could help you with that."

"But I'm still in high school," I said, doubting myself.

Spencer encouraged, "So, who says you can't branch out right now and start your dream? I'm just saying, you're beautiful, and I already know you're smart. You don't take any mess off of any-body, but you've got a big heart. Go get yours! Be business sophisticated."

CHAPTER FOUR
SECRET

"So do you have a boyfriend or what?" I said to my sister Ansli after school as I saw her waving good-bye to Hugo.

"I know, right!?" she said, as we both screamed.

We knew we didn't have a lot of time to talk about it. All our siblings will be out at the car in no time. I wanted to drive to school, but my dad insisted on the first day he'd pick us up. Again, I didn't know if it was a publicity stunt to show that he was the best dad in the world and to show his constituents that he truly supported public schools or if it was because he loved us. However, as soon as I saw him with his arms open wide, although I wasn't in kindergarten anymore, I knew it was because he loved us. No cameras were around, no reporters, no witnesses, just a father happy to see his girls.

"Don't you say anything to Dad either. This is between us," Ansli tugged on me and whispered.

"I got you."

"See you later, Shelby," Spencer said as he came from nowhere and headed toward the parking lot.

"Wait, isn't that that joker... he's Mr. Brown's son? The troublemaker goes to school here?" my dad said.

Insulted, I defended, "He's not a troublemaker, Dad. If you just let me explain."

"You know what I told you. I'm not getting into anyone else's family drama, but I saw the way he was looking at you and the way you were looking back at him. His butt can't do nothing for you but keep on walking," my father voiced.

I was so irritated. My dad had Spencer

pegged all wrong. He wasn't a hothead. He was actually quite level-headed and actually had me thinking about my future.

When my three other sisters came out of school, my dad became preoccupied because the chatterboxes, particularly Sloan, wouldn't stop going on about the day.

That gave Ansli the chance to tug on my ear and say, "So you didn't text me and tell me Spencer was here. Y'all were making goo-goo eyes. What is going on?"

"Nothing. He is just cool, and I don't want to talk about this now."

"Oh, no need to talk later. No secrets between us, Miss Thang."

***

Later after dinner, I was helping my mom straighten up the kitchen. We had a maid, but she was off on Mondays. Spencer's idea would not leave my brain. I needed to chat with her.

"Mom, why do people always say, 'Do you know what you want to be when you grow up?' Like why do you have to grow up to know what you want to be? Is it silly for a young person to start their career before they go to college? Is a degree the only thing that says one is qualified to pursue her dreams?"

She stopped cleaning and squinted my way, "It's just something we say. I guess more times than not, adults don't want kids to grow up until they have to. But if there's something deep inside of you yearning to come out, there's absolutely nothing wrong in going for it. And when I think about it, most kids don't really think about their future until the last minute. Why are you asking all of this? You ready to be my lawyer?"

"Mom, come on. That's *your* dream for me."

"I just want you to go after something sensible. A lot of kids have pie-in-the-sky dreams. Like Slade wanting to be a singer. If you ask most African American males, they want to play sports. I mean come on. There're not many Rihannas and LeBron Jameses out there, but every state and every city has tons of attorneys, doctors, and educators. I just thought you would want to take over your dad's practice one day, that's all."

Yes, I was inquisitive. And yes, I helped my mom step up her attorney wardrobe, but not because I was interested in the profession. She completely misunderstood. I just got tired of seeing attorneys so uptight. Suits could be fun. Splashes of colors here and there, the right cut, the right fit, the right tug, the right snug. She just needed glamorizing, and I helped. I had a gift, and I guess it was eating me up that I had to keep it to myself because my mother didn't think I could make a living pursuing it.

"Why don't you go start your homework?"

"It's the first day of school, Mom. We don't have any homework."

"Well, read ahead. We've always talked about that. That's another thing that kills me with kids. Just because the teacher didn't tell you to finish reading chapter 1 in whatever class you have, that does not mean that you don't need to use common sense. Follow the syllabus, and get ahead!"

"Yes, ma'am," I said a little deflated that I wasn't getting the encouragement from her that I desired.

I went to my room and, taking her advice, pulled out my government book and began reading chapter 1. Our assignment was to read it in class and answer questions, but because Mr. Freeman talked to me the whole class period, I never read it. He told me I didn't have to turn in the assignment, but my mom was right. It's best to be ahead, and I certainly did not want to be behind. So I got through the chapter. It was full of people that came here with dreams and told how our government was first started. While I thought it was jacked up how they did the Native Americans, I appreciated their passion.

I need to be able to show my mom that I could be a fashion designer. If it's what I wanted, then I needed to start now and go after it wholeheartedly. I loved my scart, but it was time for me to sketch. I had no idea what I was going to create, but I thought about the characters I met—Lyrica, Jazzy Jay, and others I passed in the hallway—and the next coolest outfit for today's modern kid went from my brain to the canvas. When the three stooges came in to tell me good night, Sloan snatched the paper away.

"You are so good," Sloan said.

"I think I want to start now, you guys. I know I want to be a fashion designer, and I want to see my clothes in the hallways."

"Yeah, everybody was loving your jacket," Slade said.

"People really liked the one I had on too," Yuri added.

"So what are you waiting for?" Sloan asked.

"I don't know. In most people's eyes, I'm still a kid."

Sloan placed her hand on her hip and said, "And? So . . . you got talent."

My cell phone was ringing. I didn't recognize the number.

"Alright, y'all, go ahead and go . . . Hello?"

"Hey. It's me—Spencer. Sorry to just call you out of the blue like this."

"How did you get my number?" I asked.

"I can't tell," he teased.

"Jazzy Jay gave it to you."

Spencer admitted, "Okay. Keep it between us though. He didn't want you to know that he gave it up. Is it alright that I called though? I saw you with your dad, and the way he was checking me out was like, 'Leave my baby alone.'"

"He'll be alright, but I wanted to thank you. It's ironic that you called because I'm going to take your advice. I'm going to let what's inside of me come out. I'm not going to keep my dreams bottled up any longer. I'm going to be a fashion designer. I'm going to be one now, and I got you to thank."

"That's what's up," he said.

And I couldn't let him know it, but the way he said it and the fact that he called and the way he looked at me when he was leaving school made my heart go pitter-patter. We had something in the making. Truth be told, that is what was up.

***

"Okay, foxy lady. You're going to be a designer. About time you made up your mind. Where have you been all my life?" Jazzy Jay said the next morning when he and I were in fashion merchandising class.

"So are you and Spencer talking now?" I

asked unsure, leaning in closer to him, wanting to know the scoop.

"And if we are, you jealous?"

"No, because obviously you're talking about me."

We laughed. He filled me in on Spencer wanting my number.

Marks High School wasn't going to be half bad. It didn't just give the basics; it had the arts, some technical pieces, and career pathway classes. I had fashion merchandising and criminal justice. Taking a law class was the only way my mother would approve my schedule. They were both electives, but for some reason, she really thought I was going to be her. She had four other daughters for that. Although I couldn't see any of them wanting to be an attorney either. I just wanted her to lay off of me. Let me forge my own trail. Let me make my own way. Any person in her right mind knew most attorneys in America had stable jobs and great incomes. That profession was a promising career that yielded great results; however, being a lawyer was not in me. She didn't need to push it. The only way I could show her that I was destined to do something else was to take my dreams seriously and believe in myself even if no one else was.

"So what's up? We're sitting here waiting on the teacher to come in the classroom, so are you going to be a designer or what?"

"I mean, I want to . . ."

"Yeah."

"But I don't know how. I need a mentor or something."

"Well, that's what I was hoping you'd say, but don't sweat it. After school let's swing by to visit my cousin."

"I don't know," I said, forgetting that his cousin was the hottest up-and-coming fashion designer in the South.

"So you don't want to meet Sydnee Sheldon? The new Gloria Vanderbilt, Bill Blass, and Guess of our time, who's got the hottest jeans out, baby."

Thankfully, Ansli and I both drove today. We have twin Chevy Sonics except hers was a hatchback, and mine was the standard four-door. Hers was red, and mine was white. There was a yearbook staff meeting after school, and she wanted to get into some activities. My other siblings would have to wait on her so I could go with Jazzy to meet Sydnee.

"How do you know she'll help me? How do you know she'll talk to me?"

"Because I already set it up, boo. Don'tcha know who ya talking to? I don't play. Just tell me what you need, and Jazzy Jay can get it indeed. Alright . . . alright!"

"You all need to settle down. This is a classroom full of seniors not kindergartners," Ms. Anderson, our teacher who looked like she had anything but style, came in the door and said. I couldn't get any more from Jay for the rest of the class.

***

"Give me that thing around your neck," Jazzy Jay said to me as we were walking into the cafeteria.

"No," I voiced as he proceeded to try to take it.

"You want to sell some, don't you?"

Realizing he was serious, I took it off, and he put it on. He wasn't wearing it any way that I would have preferred, but it still looked darn good. He was walking as if he was on a runway, and a whole bunch of people's heads were turning.

"How much you selling them for?"

"I don't know."

"Well, you better come up with a price."

"Twenty."

"Too high. Ain't none of us workin'."

I said quickly as I calculated that I'd still have a profit, "Ten."

"Sweet. I want a dollar for every one of them I sell."

"Okay," I agreed, and he pranced away.

I was alone at the table until Spencer came up. "Is this seat taken?"

"Jazzy will want it, I'm sure."

"Please, he's too busy trying to make a dollar."

"Well, sit then."

"So, he texted me and told me you two were going to meet his cousin," Spencer said, showing interest.

I teased, "You better watch it. You two are getting mighty close."

"It's cool. He knows I have my eye on another," Spencer said, looking deep into my eyes.

I had to take a very deep breath. That moment froze in my mind the rest of the day. I should have been so excited getting to meet a twenty-five-year-old designer who was taking the fashion industry by storm, but I couldn't help thinking about Spencer. He said his eye was on somebody, and his eye was locked on me. The rest of the day was a blur.

***

"Earth to Shelby! Come on. Let's get out of the car. We're here," Jazzy Jay said when I drove to Sydnee's downtown brownstone. "Hurry up. She's waiting on us. Come on."

"So this is Shelby Sharp. I'm so excited to meet you," Sydnee said as she let us in to the immaculate store.

She took me around and was really nice. She was way taller than me. I don't see how she was related to Jazzy. She was on point. She had it all together, but why was she sort of fawning all over me?

"I'm just going to be real. I've got a big fashion show coming up in a couple of weeks, and when Jazzy Jay called me and asked if I wanted to meet you, I thought, 'That'd be great!'"

"You did?"

"Yes! Because, cutting straight to the chase, I need your help. Your dad is going to win mayor. I want to get on his side now. If he can come to my event now and bring the press with him . . . ahh that just ups my stock. Can you help me?" Sydnee asked.

The only thing I could think of was Spencer saying in my ear, "See, here is one of those opportunities. Somebody needs something from you, but you need something from them . . . work it, leverage it, get what you need."

"I can do that if you mentor me," I blurted out.

Her shrewd eyes looked me up and down. I guess she underestimated me, but she stuck out her hand and said, "Done."

Now, I had created a problem. How in the

world was I going to get my dad to the show without him knowing what I was doing? Ugh, what have I gotten myself into?

***

"Hello?" I said when I picked up the phone later that evening, excited to see it was Sydnee Sheldon's number. "Ms. Sheldon?"

"You can call me Sydnee. I just wanted to tell you it was great meeting you, and I wanted to see if I could talk to your dad to give him any details he might need about my fashion show."

A lump went into my throat at that moment. I hadn't even mentioned it to my father. Was she serious?

"Is he around? I know I'm catching you on the spot, but I believe in getting things done."

One thing I was learning about people who were entrepreneurs is that they weren't shy. If you wanted something, you had to go after it, but I wasn't planning on telling my dad what was up. I just want to get him there, and once he was anywhere where cameras were, he would do his thing and deliver. But now, she wanted to talk to him?

"Well, maybe when I come next time to hang out with you, learn the business, stuff like that, you could talk to him then."

"No, I need to talk to him before then. Your mom or somebody. I'm not just going to work with you and not have your parents aware we have a deal. I need to make sure that deal is in place. I can't tell you how many people I hooked up with who didn't hold up their end of the deal."

"I wouldn't do that."

"I know you wouldn't intentionally do that, but if I'm going to be telling people your dad is coming, putting his name on posters and stuff, then I need permission to use his name and likeness. Is there going to be a problem with that, Shelby?"

In so many ways there was a big problem with that, but I had to keep cool. I had to figure this out. The only thing I could say to her was, "I'll get back to you."

"Okay, don't come back around here until you do. I hate to sound curt, but this is business, you know?"

As soon as I hung up with Sydnee, I went into my dad's study. "Dad, how's the campaign going?"

"You're mighty chipper. What do you want, Shelby Grace?" he asked, knowing me. He always called me Shelby Grace when he knew I was up to something.

"Go ahead and sit down, Shelby. I'm working, honey. Talk to me ... tell me what you need."

In a low tone, I said, "Well I did something."

"Well, what did you do?" he said, giving me a look.

"I didn't do anything horrible. I mean, it's sort of horrible because I didn't talk to you first, but I'm going for my dreams, Dad, and I know you'd do anything to help me with them, so ... it sort of isn't that bad."

"Okay, you're talking all around the edge of this. Give me the point."

"I want to be a fashion designer, and I met Sydnee Sheldon, the lady ..."

Cutting me off, he surprisingly said, "I know

who she is. She's got new jeans that everyone is trying to get in their stores."

"Exactly! Dang, Dad. You're hip."

"She's been calling my office."

"She wants you to show up at her fashion show."

"Yeah, I just don't know if I need to get out there and endorse any businesses right now."

"See, here's the thing. I sort of told her that you were going to go."

"You did what?" He was not smiling. He was completely serious. I got up out of the chair and took a couple of steps backward toward the door.

"Shelby, what did you do?"

"Well, she wants you to come to her fashion show and has been trying to get in touch with you, and I need a mentor. Like you said, Dad, she's awesome."

I pulled out my iPhone and went to the Internet and pulled up some articles.

"You don't have to sell me on her. I know she's great."

"And so I was wrong to try to get you

committed without you're approval, but she'll only help me if you're gonna come to her thing. I need this, Dad, bad. She can help take me to another level. She's so young, and I know she gets my designs, but I know she'd only give me a chance because of who my dad is. I'm just trying to learn to leverage that. Isn't that what politics is all about? Promising things to your constituents so you can get their vote?"

"Okay," he said, cracking just a little in my favor. "I like where you're going with this. I don't see the harm in showing up. You need to clear this with your mom though."

"Thank you, Daddy! Thank you!" I said as I rushed over and kissed him really hard on the cheek and hugged him even harder.

"But do not do that to me again. Seriously, there're going to be a lot of guys coming to you girls wanting things. Particularly if I win, they will want you to get them to me. Don't let them use you, and for sure, don't use me."

I nodded. "I'm sorry, Daddy."

"Alright. Get out of here."

***

Two days later, after both of my parents talked to Sydnee and agreed I could learn from her, I was at her shop. I was super excited. Getting a chance to learn from the best was awe-inspiring.

"I love these designs," she said.

Sydnee explained that she liked my creativity, the out-of-the-box thinking, the cuts, and the lines. Also, when she went into detail explaining what she admired about my work, I knew she wasn't just blowing smoke and trying to get closer to me. I knew she was taking the mentoring thing very seriously.

"If you go in the back, I got a sketchbook that I used at your age. You're much further ahead than I was. You might have to look through a couple of boxes, but be careful, and please don't fall down. It's on the top shelf in the back room. When you see what I did compared to what you do now, you'll see you are far better than I was at your age. You got skills, Shelby."

I was so enthusiastic that I was with her. Just

being in her presence, being in her back room, and seeing her fabrics and current sketches made me giddy. Being a part of that creativity was mind-blowing, but now I had to find a book. Not that I wanted to toot my own horn, but I couldn't believe her sketches were as bad as she was saying they were. But the fact that she was even giving me the privilege to look at them was super fantastic.

Then I heard some scuffling and a male voice getting extremely loud. I peeked out of the curtain, and a guy who was all hugged up with her was now in her place of business growling like a grizzly bear ready to devour her for his dinner or something.

"I gave you five hundred dollars yesterday, Brian. I'm not giving you any more cash. I need it all for the fashion show."

And then I saw this Brian guy take his hand and throw a rack of clothes to the ground. She started shaking, and before she could run away, he grabbed the back of her shirt, turned her around, and punched her. Sydnee Sheldon, the great up-and-coming fashion designer, didn't have a perfect life after all. She had an abusive man in her life. I'd stumbled into another horrible secret.

CHAPTER FIVE
SENSUAL

Brian raised his arm to hit her again, and my heart stopped. I had to make a decision. I wasn't a punk. I wasn't going to stay in the shadows and allow her to get beaten to a pulp, but if I went out there, who's to say he wouldn't hurt me too? I was looking for my phone, but it wasn't on me. I had a bad habit of putting it down, and everywhere I put it wasn't where I needed it.

"No, no! Brian!" Sydnee hissed. "I'm not alone here. Please, calm down."

"What do you mean you're not alone?"

"I've got a new girl. I'm mentoring her."

"A girl? You're lying. You're here by yourself. You're always here by yourself. I helped make you. I put off all my hopes and dreams just so you could have a future, and then as soon as you get some notoriety and some checks, you can't pay me back?"

"I'm not alone! I'm not alone! I swear," Sydnee said with severe despair in her voice.

"She's not alone," I yelled out as I came from behind her curtain.

Brian licked his nasty lips and smiled showing his gold tooth. "Ooh, you've got a pretty young thang in here."

"Brian . . . Brian, please just go. You don't want to mess with this girl."

"You don't want to give me any money. You need to make me happy one way or another," he said, eyeing my thighs like he wanted to touch them.

"Just tell him who I am already," I said, wishing I could take back the way I said it.

I was appalled by this guy. Didn't he know who he was messing with? This was Sydnee Sheldon. She didn't need him. He might have helped her when she had nothing, but now she had something, and she didn't need him. And if she needed me to stand up to him and speak on her behalf, I was ready to do that.

Brian looked confused, but he didn't release his tight grip on her.

"Her dad's running for mayor. He'll be here in a second. We don't need any trouble," Syndee said.

Brian stepped back and started shaking, clearly nervous like his tail should be. "I need to have a talk with her. I need to make sure she's not going to go tell her dad what she thinks she saw."

When he turned to walk toward me, Sydnee yelled out, "She didn't see anything, baby. She didn't see anything really."

Sydnee stepped in front of him. She started kissing on his neck and rubbing hard on his back. Her fingers started unbuttoning her blouse all in an effort to keep his attention on her.

"Don't think about anything but me right now, baby. Here . . . here . . . I will give you the money." She went over to her safe, but the Brian creep was looking at me like I was his girlfriend.

"What's your name, girl?" he said, showing me he was not in complete control of his faculties.

I realized Brian had to be on something. I wasn't quite certain what someone looked like when they were high. However, the slurred speech and droopy eyes were sure indications that something was going on with him.

"This ain't enough!"

"That's all I got right now, baby. I'll meet you a little later on. Let me just finish up with her, okay? Go home. Let me just finish up. Go home."

She was begging him, and I did not understand. I was here to learn from her, but the way she was acting with this man was certainly nothing I wanted to emulate. Then finally, after breaking her heart and some of her things, he left.

An emotional Syndee started crying. "I'm sorry you had to see all that. Ever since he lost his job a month or two ago, things have just been crazy."

"But he hit you! Was it the first time? Why do you let him? Why is this okay?" I asked.

She snapped, "You wouldn't understand, okay? And he didn't hit me."

Now, she was brash with me, which was crazy because I saw what I saw. I wasn't going to let her talk herself out of what was real, but before I could talk to her anymore about him, the nut was pounding on the door.

"Is he back?" I questioned, truly fearful.

The only thing I could do was think I needed to find my phone. I needed to call the police. This whole situation was inane.

I saw an object in his hand. "You can't let him in. He's holding something. We gotta call the police."

"You can't call the police. If they come and get him now, he could go away for a long time. He's on probation, okay?"

"You are dating some kind of ex-con?"

"So what if I am? Don't judge me. All of us weren't born with a silver spoon in our mouths."

Pissed, I defended, "You act like doing the right thing is easy too. I make choices."

Lashing back, she said, "I don't have to help you."

"Well, my father doesn't have to help you."

"Okay, okay, let me just take care of Brian, and then we can talk about this, okay?"

"If you let him in here, we're done."

She looked at me like she wanted to scream, but she understood I was serious. I was not going to agree to let his unstable behind back in. I looked out the window and confirmed he had a gun. He had a temper. He was on something.

"You can't come in here, baby. Her dad is on the way, and you know he has a police escort and all. You've got to go!"

Brian screeched, "I-I just need you to give me a few more dollars. This isn't enough."

"Okay, I'll do it later, but you got to go now."

A siren rang down the street, and I guess that spooked him because he left. Sydnee sank to the floor. She grabbed her head and shook it in pain.

I went right up to her and said, "You can't stay with this man."

She looked at me and rolled her watery eyes,

"Just please stay out of my business, Shelby. I love him!"

***

I actually was excited to get out of Sydnee's place and be with my family even though we were being scrutinized. My mom and my dad didn't always get along, but they had healthy arguments. Watching him open the door for her, hold her hand, and ask her for her opinion, I thought that should be the standard for relationships around the world. I now knew firsthand that that wasn't the case, so I appreciated, even more, what I had as my example.

My father had a passion for his family, for his wife, and for his girls, but when I was at the town hall meeting, something inside of me thought, "Dad isn't digging deep enough." He wasn't letting everyone know the true Stanley Sharp. I couldn't put my finger on it, but I thought his answers and the answers of the other candidates were subpar at best.

We were at the Panthers' stadium, and lots of people were there because the Panthers' training camp had just ended. There was a big crowd for the town hall meeting. A long line of folks were ready to ask the candidates questions, and every answer from all three of the candidates just seemed too rehearsed.

For example, a question came to Mr. James: "What do you plan to do differently to take Charlotte to a higher level?"

Mr. James said, "I plan to better the education system, better our economy, and better the welfare of the great citizens of the city of Charlotte." But Mr. James wasn't specifically saying how he was planning to better education, but he did say how he planned to make Charlotte a more profitable town. Also, he did not describe what issues he was going to focus on to help the people.

Mr. Brown was asked, "Do you feel like the city employees deserve a raise?"

He didn't even answer the question. He boasted, "As long as I'm in office, all of the decisions made by my team will be transparent."

And when my dad was asked about crime, he responded, "I'm deeply concerned that crime is on the rise in Charlotte, but if I'm elected mayor, it will go down."

How was he planning to get crime down? What was he going to do differently? I wasn't moved by any of the candidates.

"Why are you frowning?" Sloan drilled me.

I didn't even realize my sister was watching me so closely. I certainly wasn't trying to make it seem like I didn't like what my dad said, even though I didn't like the answers my father was giving at all. I huffed, trying to control my disappointment.

"Dad seems nervous, huh?" Sloan asked me even though that's not what I was saying at all.

"I'd be nervous too," Yuri leaned in and shared. "This stadium is half packed like it is for a football game."

"If Dad wants to be the mayor, he can't be nervous though," Sloan said.

My mother wasn't around. She had to sit up a little closer with the wives. Taking charge, I shushed my sisters.

Sloan corrected, "You're the one who made me say something, giving looks like everything

Dad's saying is ridiculous."

"I just want him to do well. Don't read any more into it," I leaned in and told her.

And just when I needed him to step up his answers, he was asked a question about education. "Sir, you've had your daughters in private school for years, and all of a sudden, you moved them to public school. Should we believe you're sincere?"

My dad answered, "Well, I think parents with children have hard decisions to make when they decide which type of schooling they want for their kids. Public school, private school, and homeschool all have their own positives and negatives. Some people never think private school is wrong, but many of you are aware that the private school my children were in lost its accreditation. Yes, we could've gone to another private school, there're several great ones in the city, but we've got some excellent public schools too. If I'm elected mayor of this great city, I would have great influence with our school board. And since my children needed a change, I thought the best way to be able to give advice is to be in the trenches and to be like the majority of parents in our city. Our school system is on the upswing with Common Core standards. Many states are chasing North Carolina. I'm sincere in wanting the best for my children, and the best for them is a public education."

Another reporter grilled, "So you would suggest public schools to parents now? It's only been a couple of days. How do you know your girls like it?"

My father confidently continued, "My daughters are very vocal. Trust me. If they hated it, I would know and so would you, but I want to run this city from the heart. If the public school system is good enough for my children, then I think it's good enough for anyone else's here. But if parents choose to do something else, I fully support that. We just want our young people to have the best. We want them to love Charlotte like we do so that they get a higher education and give back to our community so our futures will be intact."

Now, my dad was talking. He was getting cheers and tons of support. People could feel his passion, and if he stayed in that place, he'd win. And better than winning, he'd do a great job.

***

"Wait, wait, wait. Where are you going, baby?" I heard Fritz say, as I was walking toward my locker because my teacher let me get something out of it. I didn't want to answer him, so I just kept walking, and of course, I heard footsteps behind me. "You don't have to switch that hard for me. You should know I like what I see. You ain't got to respond, but I see in your swing you like me watching."

"Okay, where are you getting all this from?" I finally turned around and said. "I'm going to my locker to get something. Don't you have a girlfriend?"

"So if I didn't have one, you and me could get . . ."

"No, no, no," I quickly cut him off and said. "You and me couldn't get nowhere."

Then he started licking his lips. He worked his pelvic area like that was gonna turn me on. I turned around so quick and dashed to my locker.

"Hold up, baby. You ain't got to be scared of big poppa. I know you left me this love note." He actually pulled out a folded-up piece of paper. "Dear Fritz, let me lick you down . . ."

"You don't have to read any more. I didn't write that."

"Yes, you did, baby. Come here," he said, coming closer.

He was so creepy. I didn't even want him to know where my locker was, but it was too late for all that. Any other time there would be teachers, administration, the school resource officer, somebody patrolling the hallways to make us hurry up and get to class. However, we were the only two isolated there, and he was trying to take full advantage of that.

"Could you back up so I can open up my locker?" I said, trying to be cool to see if that would make him take a hint.

"Just tell me the truth about this letter. Tell me how you really feel. My boys said they've been seeing you watching me," he continued, being as delusional as a *D* student thinking he could go to Harvard.

"What are you talking about, Fritz? Aren't you hearing me? I don't want you." But he took his hand and put it on my butt. I shouted, "Okay, straight up you're crossing the line. Don't you see those cameras up there?"

"Everyone knows the cameras in this school aren't working yet. They've been having technical difficulties. Nobody's watching us, baby. Is that what you're worried about?"

He leaned in and tried to kiss me, and before I could slap him, someone called his name really loud. "Fritz! What are you doing? Why are you on her like that? Didn't she just say stop?"

I was so happy his girl, Lyrica, walked up. I'm sure she knew he was roaming the hallway, so she needed to find him before he found some girl to come on to. Fritz eased back and gave me breathing room.

"I'm going to let the two of y'all talk. Excuse me," I said as I went around him.

He grabbed my hand. "What are you doing? She knows she got to share me."

"Fritz!" Lyrica cried out.

I jerked my hand away. As soon as I got

around the corner, I hit myself in the head. I hadn't even gone to my locker. I needed to get my phone and my homework for government. When I went back around the corner, I couldn't believe Fritz had Lyrica up against my locker so tight. His right hand was around her throat, and his other hand was up her skirt.

"Listen, don't embarrass me in front of any chicks at this school. You're my girl, but not exclusively. You know what they say. A man's got to do what a man's got to do. Stop following me, and you won't catch me, but if you do, you better look the other way."

"I don't want to share you," she sobbed, sounding stupid!

"Well, you better get used to it, or you won't have me at all. Now, just relax, baby. Don't make me hurt you. I wanna make you feel good."

Lyrica whimpered, "Stop. Not in school like this. Not in school like this! I don't wanna have sex now."

He tightened his grip around her throat. I gasped when I saw him take her head and bump it hard against the locker.

"I'm the man in this relationship. I wear the pants. I tell you how it's going to go. I'm never letting you go, baby. You're mine."

"Stop, Fritz. Stop."

"Oooh, I like it when you squirm like that. Do we have an understanding? I know you like it forceful," Fritz said as he jerked her panties down.

"Stop it, Fritz," Lyrica could barely yell out.

I couldn't tell if he was actually raping her or if he was hurting her more. Whatever he was doing was wrong, but did she really like it? I was confused when he said, "Dang, Lyrica, I knew you wanted me. That's it. Relax. You so sexy and sensual."

CHAPTER SIX
SANCTUARY

"Stop, Fritz, stop!" Lyrica said over and over.

But he wasn't stopping, he just kept pressing his body up against hers all hard, and he wouldn't move his hands from around her neck and from under her skirt. Without thinking about the consequences, I finally had enough, rushed over, and hit him.

"Stay out of this! This is our business!" Lyrica, surprisingly, had the nerve to say to me.

"Did you just hit me?" Fritz got overly angry and grunted out.

Taking up for me, Lyrica shouted to Fritz,

"Leave her alone. She was trying to help me."

"Naw, she gon' get all up in my business. She shoulda kept walkin'. The hefa thinking she all betta than everybody!" Fritz bellowed as he raised his hand to hit me.

It was all happening so fast the only thing I could do was shut my eyes to brace myself for the blow. Thankfully nothing came. I heard grunting as a firmer, tougher grip grabbed him and punched him in the gut. Spencer had come out of nowhere. He and Fritz were tussling, going at it, and fighting right in front of my face.

I went over to Lyrica and said, "I couldn't stay out of it. You were telling Fritz to stop, and he wouldn't."

"I know how to handle him. I know how to keep Fritz calm. But now, you just pissed him off. This was none of your business," Lyrica disputed.

"He was assaulting you. Anybody who's sane and noticed what was going on wouldn't just keep moving. I had to help make sure you were okay."

She pointed at the guys. "I said I was alright!

Now, you got this fool fighting my man!"

"For you!"

"Like I asked for help! And if you wouldn't have walked around here trying to get the attention of every guy in the school, we wouldn't be in this mess anyway," she accused.

"Are you serious right now, Lyrica?" I rolled my eyes and asked, wanting to snap the crooked, wavy weave out her dang head and knock some sense into it. "He's a jerk. The fact that you allow him to put his hands on you like that and you call him your boyfriend knowing he's chasing every chick in this school makes you either desperate or insecure."

She shoved me. And I really wanted to punch her then, but she'd already been violated. She was supposed to be on my side, and now, she was mad at me because I was coming to her defense. Forget her.

Last thing I wanted was for Spencer to get in trouble. When I heard a whistle blowing over and over, I knew he needed to stop, calm down, get up, and stop fighting. He and I were new to this whole system. Yes, the school was new, but the principal came from the same school where the majority of the students at this school went. Fritz and Lyrica went to the old school. I'd seen them in the hallways shaking hands with the principal. And yeah, the principal was cool with me because of my dad, but Spencer already had a label on his back. I just didn't want him to get into any more trouble.

I yelled, "Stop! Stop, Spencer, I said! Let's just go! The principal is coming . . ."

But Fritz was holding onto his shirt. He wouldn't let him go. Fritz couldn't fight him and he couldn't beat him, but now that an administrator was coming, he wanted to make sure Spencer got caught.

"Let go of me, man!" Spencer said with his hands in the air.

"What's going on here?" our principal came up and questioned.

Dr. Garner said, "You two get up. Get up right now!"

Fritz put his hands in the air. "It wasn't me, sir. You know it wasn't me. I got to play on Friday night, and I'm not trying to lose my spot 'cause of no chump. He was messin' with my girl, put his hands on her and stuff. When I told him to back away, he socked me, and I ain't no punk, man. You know I ain't no punk."

"That's not what happened at all!" I yelled, utterly disgusted with the lies.

I looked at Spencer like, "Say something." But he said nothing. It wasn't even like he was trying to defend his actions. He came to my aid, and he wasn't even saying anything to help himself.

Dr. Garner added, thinking he had the right guy, "You just need to go on back to class, Miss Sharp. Come on, young man, let's go into the office. I don't tolerate any fighting here."

"So you just gon' take his word? You just gon' believe him?" Spencer said.

"You're not saying anything. You're not defending yourself," I said, hot with outrage. When Spencer looked defeated, I turned to the principal. "I'm waiting for you to ask me what happened!"

"Come on now . . ." Fritz looked at the principal and defended, "you know I can't get suspended, or I won't be able to play. We got to win. The first game ever going down as a loss in the history books if you take me off the team. It went down like I said; ask Lyrica."

"Yeah, ask Lyrica," I concurred, knowing she wasn't going to let Fritz get away with it.

But she walked away saying, "It happened just like Fritz said."

I ran up behind her and said, "No way, no way, you're gonna lie? You can be mad at me all you want, but you're not going to let Spencer get in trouble because we were helping you!"

"But I didn't ask for your help! How come you don't get that?" Lyrica shouted.

Frustrated, I said, "We were coming to your aid! You couldn't handle it by yourself. You don't even need to be with Fritz. He's crazy."

"Who's crazy now? Your boy Spencer is going to the office? Bye-bye!"

"Miss Sharp, get on to class!" The principal yelled out.

But how could I go to class? How could I leave? How could I be okay with Spencer getting in trouble? This reminded me of a couple of weeks back when he got in trouble for the wrong reason. He was always there to help me, and now, there was nothing I could do to help him. Yet again, Spencer's punishment just wasn't right.

***

I was in government, but I couldn't stay there. It just wasn't feeling right to me to not go to the office and speak up on Spencer's behalf. I mean, I said something; I tried to get the principal to listen, but just because he didn't the first time didn't mean I couldn't make him.

"Urgh, Jazzy Jay, feel my head. I don't feel good. I got to go home," I said to my friend when Mr. Freeman came near our desks.

"It's almost the end of the day. It's almost time to go home anyway," Jazzy Jay felt my head and gave me a crazy look. "You seem fine. Besides, you can't go home! I got a whole bunch of orders for your scarts."

Excited that he really loved my designs, I said, "Oh, you said it right!"

"Who doesn't know what a scart is? If they

don't know, they not in the know. Hello!" Jazzy Jay said before he snapped his fingers.

Mr. Freeman stood before me. "Did you see Spencer out there in the hallway? He said he had to go to the restroom shortly after you left, and he hasn't come back."

"I, I, I need to go to the nurse. I feel horrible," I said quickly, remembering I had to help Spencer out.

"You look okay to me," Jazzy said, still not getting the point.

He was supposed to be my dog, my refuge, my buddy who had my back. We hadn't known each other that long, but we were kindred spirits. He was blowing up my phone about all the orders he had for the scarts, and I didn't think he was using me. He was just a businessman, and I did need a big-time salesperson. I wasn't one to get out there and flaunt what I had. Every class period he was modeling a different scart, and before that class period was over, it was sold. And although he wanted to talk to me more about what he needed from me, I needed him to get on board and tell the teacher I looked bad. So I eyed him down.

He squinted, frowned, and then smiled because he had an aha moment. Jazzy Jay said, "Well, now that you say that, turn to the left a little. Your eyes are a little puffy. Your nose drooped some two centimeters to the left. You got a lazy eyebrow . . . Okay, you don't feel good. School's almost over, you can't make it until the end of the day?"

"Nu-uh, women stuff."

That always worked on a man, and sure enough, before I could blink, I had a pass from Freeman.

"If she doesn't feel good, can I walk her to the nurse's office just to make sure she doesn't pass out or anything? Because you would hate for her to pass out and it be on your head," Jazzy Jay said to our teacher.

"Fine, but you come right back!" Mr. Freeman said as he walked over to his desk.

Jazzy Jay leaned in. "What's going on with you? Spencer ain't come back . . ."

"I got to get to the office. I don't have time to explain this."

"Explain what? I need to know. Don't hold out," Jazzy Jay snapped.

To get him off my back, I quickly said, "He was fighting in the hallway, and the stupid principal came and took him to the office."

"Fighting? And I missed it? Did his shirt get taken off?" Jazzy Jay joked.

"Jazzy!"

"No, I'm serious. And don't forget the Jay," he reminded, and I nodded. "Who was he sparring with?"

"It was Fritz."

"Oh. I hope he killed that wannabe beast."

"He did, and that's all the principal saw."

"So what you gon' do?" Jazzy Jay asked, looking at me crazy like I couldn't do a thing.

I just shrugged my shoulders but headed out determined to try. When we got to the nurse's station, which was right next to the office, I tried to go in the office door. Spoiling my plan, the nurse was standing out there waiting on me.

"Your teacher called down. I wanted to make sure you got here okay. I've already called your dad. He's on the way here," the nurse said.

"You called my dad? I'm going to be . . ." I cut myself off before I said the word *fine*.

"You're going to be what?" The nurse probed, checking me out as if I was faking. "Come on in here and lie down."

"No, no, I have to get something from the office," I blurted out, scooting by her, not giving her a chance to hold me back.

When I stepped into the office, it was crazy. I couldn't find Spencer, but I saw the principal standing there listening to a man argue with Mr. Brown and Spencer's mom. The man was an older image of Spencer, so I knew that was his father.

"You guys didn't have to come," Spencer's father said in a heated tone. "I'm the guardian right now. The school called me. So don't come up here acting like my son is messing up your life because you got a call from the school too."

Mr. Brown huffed, "If you and his mom knew how to make him act like a responsible human being, then I wouldn't need to be here." He looked at Spencer's mom. "You need to tell the school to take you off of stuff because we were on our way to an engagement, and we had to drop everything to come here to try to make sure your son doesn't get kicked out. Stupid boy of yours hasn't even been in school a couple weeks, and he's suspended for fighting. See, that's why I wanted him out of my house."

"But you got it all wrong! He shouldn't be getting suspended," I stepped in between the adults and boldly voiced.

"Miss Sharp, I told you to go on back to class," Dr. Garner said to me.

"I know, sir, but you have it wrong, and his parents deserve to know the truth."

"We know everything that happened," Mr. Brown said. "Besides you're the last person who needs to try and explain anything."

"Let her talk," Spencer's mom said.

But before I could say anything, the office door was opening up again, and my dad walked in. "Shelby, I thought you were sick. Why are you in the office? Hey, Brown . . ."

Mr. Brown was happy to get me in trouble. "She's in here putting her nose in other peoples' business. If I would have known your daughter was here, my stepson wouldn't have gone to school here."

"Like you can decide where my son goes to school," Spencer's father said.

"Come on, Shelby," my dad said to me, probably real irritated with me and Mr. Brown.

I stepped closer to the door, but then I couldn't walk out. "I'm a witness. A guy was about to hit me while he was assaulting another girl. Spencer stopped him. He shouldn't be suspended for that."

"Is that true?" Spencer's mother asked as she looked over to the corner. A man moved to reveal Spencer, who was standing over there all the time.

He gasped, "I tried telling y'all the same thing, but nobody wanted to hear it from me. Believe what you want to believe."

"It's true!" I reiterated. I turned to my father because he hated injustice. "Daddy, I tried to tell the principal, but he wouldn't listen."

"No, no, no, I didn't hear you say that to me. If you would have told me that, I certainly wouldn't have brought this young man in here, and I, I didn't even know, Mr. Brown, that he's your stepson. I mean, I, I, I just didn't know," the principal sputtered.

"Well, now all that's cleared up. Come on, Shelby, let's go," my dad said, still annoyed.

But I looked back at Spencer. Although I could tell it was hard for him to tell me thank you—and he really didn't need to because he helped me out in the first place—I could tell he nodded that he was happy. I was thankful that I had gotten him out of the doghouse.

***

Later that evening, after family time, dinner, and homework, I was getting ready for bed. My mom knocked on my door and came in. "Can I speak to you, sweetie?"

"Yes, ma'am."

"I want to make sure you're okay. Your dad told me about what happened at school today. A guy assaulting girls, that's a lot. Do you think your environment is safe?"

"Yeah, just one bad apple. Honestly, I love the school."

"Okay, I'm proud of you."

"I know you always tell me to mind my own business, but that was just it. Spencer helped me with my business, and if I let him get in trouble for nothing, I just wouldn't have been able to live with myself," I explained.

"Oh, Shelby, don't be so dramatic," my momma said, as she came over and kissed my forehead. "I could tell weeks back that you were intrigued by this young man, and maybe I misjudged him. Maybe he gets a hot head for the right reasons. And although he should always be able to control his temper, I am thankful he was there for you today."

I just hugged her. Finally, she was beginning to understand, but I didn't like the guy. Shoot, who was I kidding?

"For my government class, we've got to turn in a history fact. I'm going to watch the news, then turn off the TV."

"You're on it," my mom said. "Good night, sweetie. I'm so proud of you."

I turned on the news. And the newscaster was describing a horrible case of domestic violence where a man shot his wife, two young children, and his mother-in-law. My whole body got numb like I was paralyzed. At the same time, it felt like my heart was being torn from my chest. I wasn't in the house. I didn't know any of those people personally, but it was playing all in my mind as if I were a fly on the wall, witnessing this horrible incident.

I had been quiet about domestic violence far too long. What if Mr. Brown, Sydnee's boyfriend, or Fritz snapped, took their violence to another level, and ended the lives of the women they were abusing? I knew something about it, but I never did anything about it. How could I go on? I touched my throat because it was hard for me to breathe.

Just thinking about the lady being terrified for her life and for her two young children, who were innocent in all this, being gone was too much for me to deal with. I rushed out of my room, like I was in a track meet, went to the kitchen, and turned on the faucet. I needed some water badly. I needed to be revived. But this was real, and I knew other incidents could go that bad if someone didn't intervene. I put my head down and kept splashing water on my face.

As my head began to clear, I remembered hearing my father's campaign manager telling him he needed a "heartstring" issue if he wanted to make his lead insurmountable. My dad hadn't been able to give Lou a good answer. They'd ended their conversation with Dad promising to think more about it.

How could my dad not be feeling anything heavy as he thought of the city's plight? With the pain of the city on his shoulders, was he clueless to what was going on? If that was Spencer's mom, Sydnee, or even Lyrica, dead because of violence, I knew a part of me would be dead too.

The tears just started flowing as I felt for the lady I didn't know, wishing the city could have done more to help. With tears in my eyes, I went into the dining room and found my dad. "Dad, you need an issue. You need to turn on the news. Women are hurting in this city. We got big domestic violence issues going on, and there's going to be an uproar tomorrow over this man who killed his wife, her mother, and their two young children. I know several other domestic violence incidents that are equally bad. And it's not an old or young problem, a black or white issue, a rich or poor struggle. Domestic violence is hurting Charlotte. We need awareness about it. We need a place where women can go to get help. We need a male to speak out about this injustice."

"Come here, sweetie," my dad said, as he stood up and hugged me. "Your heart is golden. I hear what you're saying, and it moves me just like it does you. We've got to do something to give battered women a sanctuary."

CHAPTER SEVEN
SOMETHING

"Oooh, girl. I have some news to tell you. You're going to be so excited. You're going to make me the VP of your new company." Jazzy Jay rushed up to me as soon as I got in school.

It wasn't that I wasn't excited that Jazzy Jay was so helpful in getting the word out about my scarts. I probably had fifty at my house. In two and a half weeks, he sold all of them, and I haven't even had a chance to make any more. So, actually I wasn't excited that he was coming to me with more orders because school had started. I needed to keep my GPA high, and I hadn't even really been studying because so much has been going on.

Putting my hand up as to say not now, I uttered, "I know. I've got to fill some orders."

Jazzy Jay snapped and stopped me from walking. "No, honey. It's better than that."

"Sorry I seem ungrateful that you are helping me. Just stressed."

He nodded his understanding.

I smiled at the grace given and said, "So what could be better than you making my scarts the hottest thing around here?"

He tugged on my arm and pulled me close, like he had the real scoop that was gonna make my world. "I talked to my cousin, Sydnee. Girl, she wants to have your scarts on her runway at her fashion show. You're going to get a ton of press. She even wants to help you manufacture them, and we gonna be able to sell way more than that little fifty that I just sold. She wants to back your brand."

"Really?" I said with glee.

This was big news. Everything was all happening so fast for my design. If Sydnee was serious, I would go from nothing to something overnight.

My friend lightly jabbed me in the arm. "You gon' be a star! Okay so, after school you've got to work with her. This is going to be phenomenal!"

Jazzy Jay and I went our separate ways to get to class. I just started thinking. What was really up with this invitation from Sydnee? I wasn't comfortable last time I was at her place. While I knew my invention was worthy of being on anyone's runway and deserved garnering tons of attention, I was unsure of this gesture. Did she really, really believe in it like that? Or was this a ploy to keep me quiet about what I saw?

Thinking back on her crazy boyfriend Brian, I was still angry. Seeing what I saw was eating me up, but I would never betray her trust and tell. However, I did want to shout what was going on with Syndee from the rooftops so the world would know and so someone could intervene before her life was taken. Since I was gonna stay silent, maybe doing this with Sydnee would give me a chance to talk to her more, keep an eye on her, convince her that the guy she was with was not the guy she needed.

As Lyrica passed by me, I knew I already had my hands full in the dump-your-boyfriend department. If I wanted someone to work on, someone to help change her life, someone to help see the light, then that person was right in front of me. I was going to say something to her, but she was strolling around with all her girls trying to be all cool, laughing at stuff, and joking on other people.

When I looked deeper, I could tell there was a sadness deep within her. There had to be. She wasn't an idiot. She had a boyfriend who was a monster. How could she be happy with that? And just as I suspected, when her friends went their own way, she leaned her head back in despair. Right when I was about to catch up to her, she started walking to class again. As she turned the corner to go down a different hall, she ran smack-dab into Fritz, whose hands were all over another girl. She turned around and bumped straight into me.

"I-I'm sorry. I'm sorry," she rambled.

"Can we go talk," I said to her in a tone more caring than a grandmother would use. "I know we got class, but there's still ten minutes before it begins."

"Talk about what, Shelby?" Lyrica was not happy trying to deal with me.

Not wanting to get equally frustrated back, I sweetly said, "You just saw what I saw. Fritz doesn't deserve you. He aggressively put his hands on you and . . . last night, I saw the news and was broken when I heard about this lady who got killed by her husband." Lyrica's eyes started to water. "You saw it too?"

Dropping her head, she admitted, "Yeah, I did."

I placed my hand on her shoulder. "That's where you and Fritz are headed. You have got to deal with this now. If you don't let him know that what he is doing is not okay, he's going to do it to others. Lyrica, maybe one day he's going to grow up and become a man who's going to take a woman's life."

"The word's out that Spencer's not suspended anymore."

"Yeah, but Fritz needs to be," I told her.

There was a long pause. When Lyrica could not look me in the eye, I knew she knew I was right. Fritz strolled by with his arm wrapped around another girl and walked past us like we weren't even there.

Finally, Lyrica exhaled, gained confidence, and smiled my way. "I deserve better. Let's go to the office and set the record straight."

***

The last couple of days, Sydnee and I had been immersed in making sure we got her ready for her big fashion show. She hadn't mentioned Brian nor had I, but I was particularly happy that I didn't see him around. Had I not witnessed him attack her with my own eyes, I wouldn't believe she would even put up with anything that disturbing and degrading. She was such a strong lady.

Her big day had finally arrived. She'd actually turned the center of her store into a runway. Chairs were on both sides, and after we stepped back and took in the beautiful setup, we knew we were ready for lights, camera, and action.

She kept taking deep breaths as she worked with the models and changed out accessories. Her jeans were striking; beads down the sides and perfect fits that made the booty pop. I'd actually never seen anything like it. When she dressed some of them in my scarts, the models commented on how cute they were. At that moment, I saw for myself how nice they looked, and I felt like I was in my element. My passion was fashion. A scart today and a whole line of clothes tomorrow.

"I need to talk to you," Sydnee said as she pulled me to the back and cupped my face with both of her hands. "You've been by me this whole week. You haven't once judged me, and you know what I'm talking about. I just wanted to tell you thank you."

I gave her a big hug and said, "Well, I need to thank you for giving me this opportunity. Not just for working for you but being able to showcase my work. I'm honored, Sydnee, really."

"Y'all need to come out from back there. People are starting to pour in. I know I'm the hostess with the mostest but, Sydnee, you've got a press conference," Jazzy Jay said.

"No, she's doing the press conferences afterward," the blond-headed, blue-eyed man said.

"This is my publicist, Jazzy. He is handling all the PR and press. I've got to stay back here and get the models ready."

"Well, who's going to help me on the door?" Jazzy Jay complained.

"I'll go with you," I said, as I took him by the hand and went to take the post up front. "I'm looking out for my parents anyway."

Fifteen minutes later, when my mom got there, she pulled me to the side. "I'm so proud of you, Pumpkin."

"Really, Mom?" I asked, truly shocked. "You want me to be an attorney, and you haven't even seen my stuff on the runway."

"I'm proud of you because despite what I want, you've proven me wrong. Your sisters showed me all of these sketches of your work. I apologize for being too busy to look at them before and for wanting to make you into what I wanted you to be. You've stepped out here.

Now, we've got to get you a logo, some business cards . . ."

I interrupted her and teased, "A credit card so I can buy some fabric . . ."

She smiled and said, "No. For now, I'll keep you supplied. Or when you make a profit, save some to buy what you need."

Jazzy Jay nodded like that was a smart plan. My mom looked curious as to who the extravagant guy standing next to me was. "Mom, this is my friend Jazzy Jay. Jazzy, my mom."

He hugged her, gave her a thumbs-up on her outfit, and then said, "And, Mrs. Sharp, your baby has already made some profits. She sold out of her scarts."

My mom beamed. She gave me a big hug. It felt great making her proud.

My heart skipped a beat when I saw Spencer stroll up to the door. Jazzy was all over him like he was his date or something. Spencer was kind enough to play along, but he couldn't take his eyes off me, so Jazzy said, "Alright, so you ain't come to see me. There she is."

"How did you know about this?" I asked.

Spencer pointed at Jazzy. "I couldn't miss it. Besides, today's the day I hang out with my mom, and Mr. Brown had tickets to the fashion show. Anywhere he goes, it's trouble, but I'll make sure he behaves."

"Go on in the door," Mr. Brown said all loud, coming up behind Spencer.

I thought Mr. Brown was a horrible stepfather. Why Spencer was hanging with him at all was beyond me. But if he wanted time with his mom, I guess he had to figure a way to deal with it.

Mr. Brown touched my arm when he came past. "So I hear your dad is speaking on the program at the fashion show, trying to get a leg up on me. Well, I'm in the house. You go find him and tell him."

I jerked away and was about to do just that because you never know what Mr. Brown would have up his sleeve, but then my dad was making his way to the podium to start the fashion show.

"I'd like to thank so many of you for taking the time to come today to support this budding young fashion designer who's taking the world by storm. Her collection is called *Walking in Grace*, and I just want to say as a man who cares about the women in this great city, as a husband and a father and a mayoral candidate that we've got to step up more as men and open our eyes to what's plaguing our city. Domestic violence is real. You can watch the news, and there's one story after the other of senseless violence. Whether I win or not, Ms. Sydnee Sheldon and I have talked, and we're going to build a home that's a safe haven for abused women and children. This won't be the only home like this in Charlotte, but it's a start, an example to follow. "

People all over the room began to stand up and clap. We were all here for a fashion show, but my dad brought us to a place of caring. I was so proud of him.

***

The fashion show was a huge success. All four major television station affiliates had reporters there. They were saying excellent things.

Sydnee was being interviewed, and I was shocked when she said, "There's the newest star.

Shelby, come on up! They want to ask about the scarts."

One reporter asked, "You're just in high school. How did you decide to design?"

"Yeah, how did you think you could do it so young?" another reporter uttered.

"Well, as you guys know, I have great parents," I began, as the crowd laughed, knowing that I was the mayoral candidate's daughter. "But I just want to say to any young person out there with a dream, no matter what it is, no matter who believes in you, you believe in yourself. You have got to work hard, surround yourself with people who could help you learn, develop, and grow. Know that big dreams aren't going to be accomplished easily but understand that being young is no excuse that it can't be done. Even if you have little, make something of it. Hopefully, you're just seeing the beginning of what I'll become as a fashion designer, but today isn't about me . . . let's give it up for Sydnee Sheldon, an amazing mentor, designer, and woman!"

I said that last part because I looked over and saw Brian pushing in and trying to get her attention. If she was working with my dad for something for battered women, she had to have come to a place where she wasn't going to put up with his crap anymore. I certainly didn't want him to embarrass her. I gripped Sydnee's hand really tight so that she felt my support and knew she didn't need any guy who was bringing her down in any part of her life. She smiled my way. Sydnee answered a few more questions, and then she went into the back. I followed. Brian did too.

"I am just so proud of you, baby," Brian said with his arms outstretched.

"I told you not to come. It's over," she said to him boldly.

"You told him it was over?" I asked unable to hold back my excitement.

Brian started pleading, "I'm sorry for hitting you. I told you, I'm not going to do it anymore."

"Please leave. I already moved out. I've gone to the police. There's a restraining order on you. We're through," Sydnee uttered, as she peered over her shoulders at the many people watching, practically daring him to trip.

Brian saw the security watching him. Models and others backstage were frowning at him too. He stormed away without incident.

I hugged her. "I thought you were going to stick with him."

Before I could exit backstage, my parents were standing there giving me lots of love. It was a day like none other. Just stepping out, trying my dreams, believing I could, and making it happen felt great. Not just because people were receiving what I put out there in a positive way but because I felt good about what I put out there. I was a new entrepreneur. Everyone had to start some place, and at least I wasn't sitting on my dreams.

"I want an autograph," Mr. Brown came backstage and shouted. "Oh, Sharp, you back here actin' like you the designer. You got a little standing O, but you ain't doing nothing. Talking about a home for battered women. Women better learn to stand up and take care of themselves. Shoot, you just trying to get votes. I should've known you were going to be looking for anything to make your ratings go up."

"That was all genuine, bruh," my dad said to Mr. Brown in an irritated tone.

Almost angry, Mr. Brown huffed, "Yeah, right. Whatever. Battered women? Like anyone cares about them."

"If they need to stand up for themselves, then maybe I need to stop trying to act like our world is perfect and stand up to you," his wife said.

He gave her a look.

However, she continued, "I chose you over my son. How stupid am I? Battered women are scared to lose so much. That's why they never say anything. I commend Mr. Sharp for bringing this to the forefront, for empowering us women to stand up and not take it anymore."

"Are you saying you've been abused?" a reporter pierced through the curtain and asked.

Another reporter followed, "Have you been abused, Mrs. Brown?"

The curtain flung open. The questions started rushing in from tons of people. Mr. Brown was embarrassed, and he left. Spencer came through the reporters and hugged his mom.

I pulled my dad over to the side. "That's what I was trying to tell you a few weeks back at that first debate when you saw Spencer fighting his stepdad. It's because he had just learned this guy was beating his mom. Spencer's not a bad guy."

"Sir," Spencer came behind me and interrupted, "I hope you will give me a chance. I think the world of your daughter and just wanted to ask your permission to take her out on a date."

My dad slowly nodded and shook Spencer's hand. "I'm sorry I misjudged you, son. Seeing you fighting made me fear the worst. I guess even the best of us should know better than to believe in stereotypes. We fall prey to that every now and again. My daughter said you encouraged her to start her business. It looks like you've got your mom's back too. I've got high standards, but I don't have any problem if you guys want to go out soon. Right now, I want to take my family out to dinner. Shelby, can you say your good-byes and come on, dear?"

"Yes, sir. I'll be there in a minute."

"Go with your family. We'll talk later," Spencer said.

It was awkward as I wanted to hug him. I wanted to thank him, but just seeing him smile at me was enough. So I left with my parents.

When we got to the door, I heard Jazzy yell out from across the room, "You're leaving something!"

He was standing at the curtain with my phone. I turned back around to go get the phone I just couldn't keep up with. When I came back to the curtain, instead of Jazzy holding it, Spencer had it. Spencer pulled me back behind the curtain. "I snatched it on purpose this time because I wanted you to have to come back to me so I could ask you this question."

"What?" I said nervous and giddy all at the same time.

"Will you be my girl?"

I leapt into his arms and gave him the biggest kiss that made my insides melt like a lit candle. Who would have known that the guy who irritated me a few weeks back would now be the one who made my heart go pitter-patter? Spencer was mine.

In so many ways, my world was right. I believed in my dad as a candidate. I believed in myself as a designer, and I believed in Spencer as a guy whom I could trust with my heart. It wasn't time to run down the altar or drop my panties or anything, but truth be told, we'd gone from nothing to something.

ACKNOWLEDGMENTS

HERE IS A BIG THANK YOU to the people who help me make something of my writing and help me stay unstoppable:

To my parents, Dr. Franklin and Shirley Perry, thank you for helping me make my childhood special.

To my publisher, especially Adam Lerner, thank you for allowing me to make a fun series I believe will touch many.

To my extended family, thank you for your prayers, which makes me strong.

To my assistants Shaneen Clay, Alyxandra Pinkston, and Candace Johnson, thank you ladies for being such dedicated assistants who make my work top notch and relevant.

To my dear friends, thank you for standing by me, because your support makes me happy and better.

To my teens, Dustyn, Sydni, and Sheldyn, thank you for giving me a reason to work hard, as that makes me want to make you proud.

To my husband, Derrick, thank you for loving me so and taking such great care of us, as that makes me want to give back to you.

To my readers, thank you for giving my book a chance, as thinking of you flipping the pages makes me dig deep inside to write a moving story that will hopefully make your life better from reading it.

And to my Savior, thank you for opening doors that clearly show me You have me doing just what You want for my life. I am grateful, and I plan to make each book in this series uplifting.

ABOUT THE AUTHOR

STEPHANIE PERRY MOORE is the author of more than sixty young adult titles, including the Grovehill Giants series, the Lockwood Lions series, the Payton Skky series, the Laurel Shadrach series, the Perry Skky Jr. series, the Yasmin Peace series, the Faith Thomas Novelzine series, the Carmen Browne series, the Morgan Love series, the Alec London series, and the Beta Gamma Pi series. Mrs. Moore is a motivational speaker who enjoys encouraging young people to achieve every attainable dream. She lives in the greater Atlanta area with her husband, Derrick, and their three children. Visit her website at www.stephanieperrymoore.com.

THE **SHARP** SISTERS

Make Something of It

STEPHANIE PERRY MOORE

Better Than Picture Perfect

STEPHANIE PERRY MOORE

Turn Up for Real

STEPHANIE PERRY MOORE

Truth and Nothing But

STEPHANIE PERRY MOORE

Icing on the Cake

STEPHANIE PERRY MOORE